A Love Ignited

The Many Lives of Brandi

Book 1

By
Amy Allen

Dedication

This is dedicated mom and Rebecca – for all the help you've given with the making of this. Love you both.

.

TABLE OF CONTENTS

Acknowledgement

Images and Cover Art Illustration by Period Images, Pi Creative Lab and VJ Dunraven Productions. Cover Text and Branding by Elizabeth Bank with Selestiele Designs - http://www.selestieledesigns.com.

And a very big thank you to my mom for, well, everything.

Prologue

Outskirts of St Petersburg, Russia November 1804

The house was quiet but it wasn't even six a.m. yet. A young-looking woman lay there, having awakened from a nightmare, finding she couldn't return to sleep. Looking at the empty space next to her, she sighed. She still had a hard time believing he was gone. Letting her mind wander back, she thought about when she and her late husband Alexi met, and then married a year later. It was twenty-six years ago they met and twenty-five years ago they were married. Lexi and her cousins had found the young woman and her little brother Joshua at an Abbey between their home and St Petersburg, where they were being kept after being kidnapped. She recently found out that Lexi's mom had actually let Jim know that she and Joshua had been found and Jim – the man that was her first love and oldest best friend – was the one that was supposed to have found her and Joshua. It had only been happenstance, and pure luck, that Lexi and her cousins rode by first. As she returned to the present, she heard a knock on the door. Rolling onto her back, she wiped her eyes as she called, "Come in," wondering who else would be up so early.

A slightly older woman smiled as she stepped in the room. "I didn't wake you, did I, Brandi?"

Brandi gave what she hoped was a smile. "No, Domi, a nightmare did." Brandi had been calling the woman Domi, short for Dominique, for 26 years – since just after meeting the woman when Brandi was 16 years old in this lifetime of hers. Brandi thought of Dominique as not only a friend, but as a surrogate mother, even though Dominique was still technically her mother-in-law.

Dominique sat on the edge of the bed next to Brandi, as she had when Brandi was younger and was staying with them after being found. "Did you want to talk about it?"

Brandi sat up and leaned against Dominique before she nodded against Dominique's shoulder. A watery sigh escaped Brandi's lips, followed by sniffing. "It was what I have for memories from the monastery, but then it suddenly switched to a couple years later when Jeff grabbed me, Lexi, Marisha, and Stepan. It then skipped to last year when Jeff accosted me and Lexi when we were out riding and finished with ..." Brandi couldn't continue. The memory of Jeff suddenly there while they were out riding last year haunted her more than Jeff's kidnapping her, not just once but twice. While she still couldn't remember much from what happened during the six years she was in the monastery and she tried to just forget when Jeff grabbed the four of them and made Lexi watch what Jeff and his buddies did to her, she wondered if she would ever forget Jeff surprising them when he went at Lexi with a sword - taking Lexi's head before she or Lexi had the chance to even react. Lexi was a warlock and, like her, had been immortal, so he wasn't supposed to have died. She still didn't know if Jeff would have done worse if she hadn't gone after him with her own sword. Sitting straight, Brandi mentally shook off the thoughts. Glancing at Dominique, she cleared her throat and then said, "I'm sorry, Domi. I've really been trying to keep myself together and not break down."

Dominique loved Brandi, whom she first met when the latter was only a child, as if she was her own daughter - a maternal affection, which extended to Brandi's twin daughters, Anna and Leah. She also knew how much her son had loved Brandi and the girls, but since his death, Brandi had become almost a recluse and it was not healthy. Coming to a decision, Dominique suggested, "Why don't you take a break and go on holiday?" Dominique had planned to suggest one of Brandi's two older brothers – Mike or Eric – to go with her, but what Dominique said instead was, "Ask Jim to go with you. Go somewhere, other than into St Petersburg, you haven't ever been to or haven't been to in a while. Take as long as you want for a holiday. You know Anna, as well as your wolves, will be fine here with us." Dominique knew years ago that Brandi and Jim had a different, and special, relationship – not that Dominique ever worried that Brandi had cheated on Lexi with Jim, she knew better than that. She also knew that if the girl was going to heal and move forward, it would be with Jim, and the only way to have that happen was for Jim to also go.

Thinking it through, and surprised at the suggestion of Brandi going on a holiday and that she should ask Jim, Brandi nodded. "That's a good idea. I haven't been to London in a long time. I'll ask Jim, also. Thank you for the suggestion and for keeping an eye on Anna, and my two four-legged boys, while I'm gone."

Dominique kissed Brandi's cheek. "Try to get some more sleep. You can worry about everything else later this morning, or even this afternoon." Dominique was glad to see Brandi nod again before lying back down and closing her eyes. Gently standing, Dominique stepped to the bedroom door, glad to see Brandi fall back into an easy sleep.

Chapter 1

St Petersburg, Russia
December 1804

After a month of shopping, packing trunks, and getting ready to go, Brandi was glad they were finally starting their trip to England. She had been told to choose one trunk to be delivered to the room they would need to share, because the rest would go into the cargo area – set to the side so they wouldn't be accidentally sold. Once she chose the trunk she wanted, she was asked to wait to board until after the trunks and any goods to be sold in other ports were loaded. Because it was a merchant ship, Jim was asked to help on deck. Brandi almost laughed at that. Although it had been at least a hundred years, Jim had spent his share of time working on various ships. She knew he hadn't forgotten any of the deck duties. When it was time for her to board, she was glad that it was Jim who came to show her to their cabin.

Sitting near the porthole to watch as the ship pulled out of the port, Brandi thought back a month earlier. She had told Jim that she wanted to go away, leave St Petersburg, for a while – asking if he would join her - on the same day Dominique had suggested it to her. When he asked her why she wanted to travel now, and why she wanted to bring him, she told him about the three-part nightmare that had woke her early that morning, as well as her conversation with

Dominique after, including Domi telling her that she needed to let herself grieve and then move on. She also told him Domi had suggested she get away and then suggested that Brandi ask him to go with her. Brandi wasn't surprised that Jim agreed with Domi that it was past time for Brandi to let herself grieve over losing Lexi and then go on with her life, while not forgetting Lexi. She'd smiled some when he reminded her that Lexi was always going to be a part of her and that she would always love Lexi. When he didn't say if he would accompany her or not, she asked again, and was glad when he stated he would be happy to join her.

Although they were now out of port and all she could see was water, she didn't move, still lost in thought. If she were truly honest with herself, she knew she had actually started grieving over Lexi's death from the moment it happened, she'd just wanted to deny that it had happened while locking herself away from everyone else and being depressed. She also knew that in her darkest moments, she would have gladly traded her own life for Lexi's. She suddenly quietly laughed at herself, since in the last month while getting ready to leave, she'd found herself getting angry at Lexi for dying and Jeff for killing him. The laugh became a smile when she heard the door open. Turning her attention that way, she watched Jim step in and suddenly realized she'd finally accepted Lexi's death. She missed him, and always would, but she was now ready for whatever this trip with Jim brought.

Copenhagen, Denmark - December 1804

Brandi overheard, early in the trip, that they were heading to Copenhagen from a couple of young deckhands one of the few times she was on deck. When Brandi asked Jim, one night at dinner, why they were making that stop instead of traveling straight through to London, he told her that, because it was a Merchant ship, they only travelled so far. They were lucky that this one was going as far as Copenhagen.

Due to weather, blockades from warships, and trying to stay away from both pirates and privateers, it took them nearly three weeks to get to Copenhagen.

After being assisted off the ship by Jim, Brandi watched as he helped unload the cargo – their trunks, including the ones in their cabin, as well as all the goods to be sold. She hoped they had a little bit of time in port to be able to see what those goods were when they were taken to market.

Jim hadn't missed the way Brandi watched the cargo come off the ship. Joining her on the dock, he leaned down and kissed her, nearly groaning when he felt her melt into him. Ending the kiss, but keeping her close, he said, "I'm going to see about our next ship. If I can manage to find one that doesn't leave for a day or two, are you fine with staying and seeing what the merchants have for sale?"

Brandi had nearly sighed at the kiss. She could feel his want for her on top of hers for him nearly overwhelming her. She had no doubt he felt it too by the way he kept her close at the end of the kiss. She was about to tell him that was fine regarding their next ship until he asked about staying a day or so and then she nearly bounced. Even though she thought he could read her mind yet chose not to, he knew her very well and acted as if he couldn't read her mind at all. A smile lit her face and eyes. "That would be wonderful if you are able to."

He gave her another kiss before he pulled her fur-lined cloak around her, making sure she was engulfed in it while also letting his hands do some wandering, under the cloak, over her curves that he wanted to explore sans clothes. "I'll be back shortly, baby. Stay warm."

Brandi's smile returned as she nodded to him. She watched him walk away as both her heart rate and breathing finally started to even out. She enjoyed watching him, especially when he was walking away. He was tall – six-feet seven-inches. He was the youngest of triplets, as she was, and had been her best friend as well as someone she had loved for the majority of her life – well, since her true age of 6 years old and his true age of 16 years old. It amazed her that they had spent well over several millennia – and having her life restart five times at this point – not doing anything about being in love with each other. She wondered why she'd hadn't ever tried to read his mind, or even ask if he could read hers to find out if they were true mates. She hoped they were, that he was her second, well technically first, true mate. She also dearly hoped that they were going to be able to explore being more than just friends. Shaking off the thought of maybe finally having him, and the sudden feeling of guilt toward him concerning Lexi, she went back to watching him. His shoulder-length hair, hanging loosely at the moment, was a rich mid-brown – as both his brothers' were – but, unlike his brothers, who had golden/tawny highlights running through theirs, he had white highlights throughout his – due to being a white tiger shifter. His eyes were a piercing bright blue. The smile still on her lips turned sultry as she admired the way his clothes fit his lean but well-built body – his muscles well defined without being too much. Seeing him turn to look at her with a cocky grin had her realizing he knew she was watching him. She met his gaze as she let her eyes roam over his handsome and rugged face. The sharper sight, and hearing if she chose to use it, was something she loved about being a vampire. Her gaze could follow him and still see him, making her feel safe since she knew he'd be there faster than any mortal if she needed.

Jim had been well aware of her watching him. They were just too tuned in to each other, and always had been — whether they were true mates or not. He knew he needed to ask her and he hoped she wouldn't be able to. Before they'd left St Petersburg, he'd dropped the blocks he'd previously erected, and kept up, so he wouldn't feel everything she did as intensely since he really hadn't wanted to feel what she had toward, and with, any other man. Now, he planned on claiming this five-foot mouthy beauty who, to him, had always been his. She was his best friend, his first, and only, love, and his one true mate – even though he knew she had another true mate, a man she had loved millennia ago. The knowledge made no difference to his feelings. She was filled out where she needed to be while still only being about one hundred pounds – though he really didn't care if she was slim or not, that wasn't something that really mattered to him. After Alexi's death, she had scared Jim when she'd collapsed and had then been in a form of coma for a day or two. He'd stayed in her room – sleeping in a chair – while she'd been out. When she'd awakened, he was shocked at the change in her, though he'd also loved the new look. He thought it all looked sexy. Her hair changed from being all blonde and waist length to being floor length that was half white on the left side and half blonde on the right. Her eyes changed from both being sky blue to her left eye now being silver-white – so it looked like she was blind in that eye, and her right eye being arctic ice blue. She also now had unusual tattoo looking markings down her left side, which, from how her face and neck looked, went to her midline from head to toe. The one thing that had really given him pause, even though they didn't stay out, were the wings she now had that were a soft copper color. Her skin also looked to be a slightly darker copper color with a visible glow to it.

Unlike Jim, who was able to conceal his otherworldliness, Brandi had to rely on more conventional methods to cover her differences. Although hair styles and clothes worked for the most part, the markings on her face were not so easily hidden. Rather than try to disguise them, Brandi simply continued as though they were the most natural thing in the world, neither apologizing for them nor explaining how she came by them.

Like she knew who and what he was, he knew who and what she was. They had no secrets from each other and never had.

Not paying attention to where he was going, Jim suddenly ran into someone. Before he had the chance to apologize, he heard, "Maybe you should watch where you're going, little brother, instead of letting your mind wander." He couldn't help but grin when he looked at who he'd run into. Giving the man a hug, Jim said, "Ken! What in the hell are you doing here?" Because of something that had happened between Ken and Brandi just over one hundred years ago, well more like because of the way Ken had ended up treating Brandi, Jim was still a bit frustrated with his brother, but he was also glad to see the man.

Ken returned the hug and grinned. "I've gone straight. Have been for a few years now. I'm the captain of a merchant ship. We're picking up supplies and any passengers that want to go to the port of Southampton. What about you?" Ken was sure he'd seen someone he knew and cared about. Regrettably, they had parted on less than friendly terms, and he wasn't sure how she would react when she saw him again. He continued, "Why are you here, and did I see our Princess waiting near *The Mermaid?*" Referring to Brandi by the endearment he and his brothers always used.

"About fucking time, although it looks like you've lost a body part." Jim raised an eyebrow, then chuckled when Ken shrugged. "Well, you'll have to tell us how you lost your eye. Yep, you saw her over there. That's why I'm here, traveling with her. You wouldn't happen to have room for two more, would you? Even though our final stop is gonna be London, I'm actually trying to find us a ship to take us to England. I can worry about finding a way to London once we're in England, if necessary."

Ken didn't have to think about it. Even if he had several passengers, he would have made room for his brother and the woman he regretted hurting – and who he wanted to gain forgiveness from. "I do, as long as you don't mind being in the same cabin. Because there isn't a dock in London quite yet, we'll be putting in at the port of Southampton. You should be able to get tickets for a carriage to London from there." What he didn't say was what cabin he planned to put them in. He knew Jim was in love with her and always had been.

Jim shook his head. "One cabin is fine. We had to share from St Petersburg to here, though the captain had me helping on deck most of the time since they were keeping out of blockades as well as outrunning pirates and privateers, so I wasn't in the cabin much. We were able to have dinner together most nights, though. Going to Southampton is fine since it puts us in England and that's good to know we can get a carriage from there to London." Remembering what he'd told her he'd try to do, Jim wondered, "How soon are you leaving?"

Since he knew his brother well, Ken knew there was a reason behind the question, so he countered with one of his own. "How soon did you want to leave?"

Jim chuckled. "Tomorrow or the day after. She wanted to take a look at what was for sale in the market if possible."

Not caring that it might put him behind schedule, and that the only passengers would be his brother and Brandi, Ken said, "That is fine with me. Let's let her know you have a ship, and whose it is. And, if she doesn't throw a fit, we'll get your trunks loaded. I'd like to talk to you both for a few when we're done with that, if possible." Thinking about what Jim said about being on the Mermaid, Ken added, "Even with knowing how good of a deckhand you are, I won't require you to help on deck. Relax and enjoy the rest of the trip with her."

Jim was surprised that Ken didn't want his help. He also didn't want to ask what Ken wanted to talk to him and Brandi about, so he only gave a brief inclination of his head with regards to not needing to help, as well as Ken wanting to talk, before he turned with Ken and headed back to where Brandi stood. He knew the moment she saw Ken with him, due to the waves of anger and hurt he could feel coming from her. Because of his acute tiger eyesight, one of the benefits of being able to shift into a tiger, he could see her face darken and her eyes become slits. Since Ken was also able to shift into being a tiger, he knew Ken saw it too.

Arriving at Brandi's side, Jim leaned down to give her a kiss. Undaunted by the looks she was giving to him and Ken, as well as the slightly off kiss, Jim said, "I found us a ship. Ken has said we could take passage on his merchant ship. He has also agreed to not leave until tomorrow or the day after so you can see what there is in the market. We need to get our trunks loaded onto his ship and then he asked to talk to you and me." Seeing her start to open her mouth, he shook his head. "I don't know what about. We'll have to wait and find out." Jim thought he knew what the conversation was about, but he didn't want to guess in case he was wrong. "I'm going to help him get everything loaded that needs to be loaded." Lowering his voice, though knowing if Ken wanted to he could still hear what was said, Jim added, "I literally ran into him, baby. We were talking, I told him where we were headed and asked if he had room for us after he said he was heading to England and looking for passengers. He said he did, but said we'd have to share a cabin and go to Southampton then get a carriage to London. I told him that was fine. I think he is trying to make amends, baby. Can we give him the benefit of the doubt?"

Brandi sighed, knowing he was right. "All right. I'll reserve judgment until after we've talked to him. Do I need to stay out here while you all load the ship?"

Ken waited until then to listen to them. Using the nickname he, and his brothers normally used for her, Ken said, "Not unless you want to, Princess. Jim and I can load your trunks into the cabin you'll be using and then my crew will load the cargo into the hold. I'm sure Jim told you, but I'd like to talk to both of you. Follow us so you can see what cabin you'll be in."

A small smile formed across her lips when she saw he'd named his ship "Our Princess." She was surprised when they didn't head toward the area where their cabin on the Mermaid was located. Instead, they headed toward the area where she'd noticed the captain come from on the Mermaid. Stepping into the room behind Jim and Ken, Brandi nearly gawked. "Isn't this your cabin, Ken?"

Ken smiled at surprising them both. "It is, and it's my choice to give it to you two for this trip. Besides me and my crew, you both are it on the ship. When Jim asked if I had room, I decided you were going to be the only passengers and I also decided to give you my cabin. I don't need much room for just me."

He finished helping Jim get the rest of their trunks before he sat down at his desk, facing his brother and Brandi. Running his hands through his now loose hair, he sighed. "I'm sorry for how I previously behaved, Princess. I was jealous of the relationship you have always had with Jim and I wanted it for myself. I know ..." he raised his palm to halt the tirade he knew was about to spill from Brandi's lips. "... there's nothing you can say, that I haven't already said to myself. It was all in my head."

He paused, his next admission was harder. "Even though I don't deserve it, I also ask to be forgiven for blaming you for our daughter's disappearance. No one could have predicted or prevented it. I was just lashing out in anger and you were an easy target." Ken held Brandi's gaze while he spoke, hoping she could see it in her heart to accept his apology.

After a long moment, where nobody spoke, Brandi rose from her seat and walked to where Ken was sitting. Leaning down, she lightly rested her hand on his forearm to steady herself as she kissed his cheek.

"Thank you, Ken. It means a lot to me to hear you apologize. It would be wrong of me to not forgive you." It seemed to her that his apology was still lacking something, though she couldn't put her finger on what. Feeling his hand cover hers, she smiled as she also felt him give her hand a light squeeze.

"Thank you, Princess." He returned her kiss and smiled, albeit a little sadly, as she returned to her seat, then shook it off. Standing, he continued. "If you're hungry, I'll have Brian fix you both some lunch and then have my cabin boy bring it to you." Ken was glad he'd enlisted his other brother Brian, the middle of the three of them, to work as a chef on the ship. This way he knew he, and the rest of the crew, was getting fed well.

Glancing at Brandi and seeing her agree, Jim said, "Something to eat would be great, thanks, Ken. You sure you don't need my help?"

"Give me, well more like Bri, thirty minutes to fix something and then I'll make sure your lunch is delivered timely so you both can eat, and I'm sure for the help." With a grin, Ken left the cabin.

Brandi was partially surprised when a delicious meal was served before the thirty minutes had passed. She didn't know why she should be surprised since Ken had said Brian was doing the cooking on the ship. Brandi could tell, when she took her first bite, that Brian had added blood to hers to help her. Ken had also added a special drink to her tray that he had added his blood to that would help her body rest and heal from the stress he and Brian could sense from her – even though Brian hadn't actually saw her yet.

Jim made sure to touch Brandi's glass when the tray was sat in front of her to energize her drink that way since his brothers thought him the weaker and that his power of healing for her was through touch. Jim knew why Brandi was stressed and needed rest, but he hadn't told his brothers yet. He was actually surprised to hear Ken say Brian was on the ship. Since Jim knew both his brothers could read Brandi's mind, he wondered briefly if Ken had read her mind to find out why Brandi looked stressed and tired, or if Ken refrained, in respect for her privacy.

After they finished, they took their plates to the galley and thanked Brian, with Brandi giving Brian a hug also since she hadn't seen him in a couple years, before finding Ken to let him know they were heading off the ship to check out the market. After doing some shopping and returning to the ship, since Jim wasn't needed to help on deck, he spent the time on board locked in the cabin with Brandi.

Chapter 2

London, England
January 1805

Brandi and Jim finally arrived in London a few days into the New Year. Part of her was sad that Christmas was spent on Ken's ship but she was thankful for Ken and Brian making it special for both her and Jim.

They had only a partial day's ride from Dominique's house to St. Petersburg but from there it had been a month on board two different ships before they reached the port of Southampton. Surprisingly, nothing more than them kissing and letting their hands explore each other had happened while they were on Ken's ship between Copenhagen and Southampton. After reaching Southampton and disembarking the ship, they then caught a carriage to London. It took a week for them to reach London due to having to deal with snow and ice on the roadway. Jim thought he handled himself fairly well for the trip, since he didn't want Brandi to feel pushed into more while on board. He also felt weird at taking her in his brother's bed. When he helped her down from the carriage, Jim couldn't help but notice how Brandi was very happy to see land again, even though she didn't go as far as to kiss the ground. The thought made him quietly chuckle since he knew boats normally didn't bother her and they had gone almost directly from the ship to the carriage so she couldn't enjoy it in Southampton.

Although she missed them, Brandi was glad she'd left her wolves in Russia. She knew they'd be anxious from all the people, as well as wanting to run after being cooped up for so long. As her feet touched the ground, Brandi noticed Jim smirking. Raising an eyebrow, she asked "What? Did I do something funny?"

Jim made sure she was stable on the snow-covered ground before putting his arms around her. His smirk turned to a grin. "Possibly. Are you telling me you didn't read my mind?" Watching her shake her head, he then said, hoping he already knew the answer to the unasked question, "Then I'm giving you permission to read it. If you can."

"If I can?" Brandi had the feeling he was hinting at something, but decided to take the dare, even though he didn't specifically dare her. Keeping her gaze on his, she reached out to his mind guessing she'd have no problem seeing his thoughts. What she found was something she wasn't expecting. It was something that had happened only one time before – and that was close to five thousand years ago. She hit what was a figurative brick wall. Frowning, she tried again, still finding she couldn't. That only meant one thing. She glanced down briefly before returning her gaze to him. "I can't. Can you read mine?" She was amazed when he shook his head to tell her no. "Then that means ..." Although she didn't say it out loud, she knew it meant he was also her true mate – well, technically her first true mate, so she now had two true mates.

Jim dipped his head to her. "Yes, that is what it means. You're mine. Always have been. My mate. So, I'm not sitting on the sidelines anymore, baby. But I'm also not going to push you. If you want a proper courtship before anything happens, I'll gladly give you that."

Brandi considered his words. She should have realized it long ago, since she knew Jim could feel what she did, even if he didn't seem to feel what she did as intensely as she thought he would. It suddenly hit her. "Did you put up blocks so you wouldn't, or couldn't, feel what I do as severely?" She felt his nod against her head. "Do you still have them up?"

"No, I dropped them before we left St Petersburg. Figured it was time." Seeing her start to shiver, he asked, "Shall we walk for a bit?" Realizing he didn't know if they were staying at Alex's or elsewhere while in London, he then added, "Where are we staying? I can hire a cart to take our trunks so they aren't just sitting here"

Brandi rubbed her arms, feeling the chill. "A walk would be nice, especially if you can find someone to hire to take them. I'm not quite ready to get in a carriage yet. We are staying at the house here in town. The address is 10 South Moulton Street at Grosvenor Square." She thought back about the rest of what he'd said, including when he'd taken his blocks down. Casting her gaze downward, Brandi bit her lip and schooled her features, knowing the smile she planned to give him would belie what she was about to say. She hoped he wouldn't challenge her since she had never ever lied to him nor stretched the truth, in the too many millennia to count that they'd known each other. Brandi lifted her gaze, the smile now on her face turning sultry. "I would like a proper courtship."

Jim burst out laughing. Shaking his head while still laughing, he stepped to the edge of the walkway and hailed a cart he saw going past. Calming enough to talk to the man, he was able to hire the driver to take the trunks to the house, giving the man the address, and gaining the man's promise he would stay until they arrived. Jim wasn't sure if there were any servants at the house to receive the trunks, so asking the man to wait ensured their belongings would remain safe. After helping load the cart and paying the man, Jim turned to look back at Brandi only to start laughing all over again. Putting his arm out to her, the laugh quieting and turning into a grin, he was happy when she lightly took it. Resting his hand on hers, bringing her closer, he gazed down at her. Because Brandi's smile told a different story than her words, he said, "Sure, baby, but a proper courting is what I'll give you until you let me know differently." Leaning down, he whispered in her ear, "Just know, though, I plan on showing you not just how much I love you, but also how much I want to both fuck you and make love to you each time I kiss you."

Brandi sighed on a giggle at what he said. By the gods, she wished she hadn't said she wanted him to properly court her for now. Gazing up at him, she gave him the best innocent look she could and asked, "Care to show me now?"

Jim chuckled. "Which one, little girl?"

Brandi couldn't help but giggle more. Even despite the fact they were on a public street, she said, "All three?"

Growling low in his throat, Jim moved so he was standing directly in front of her. Slipping his free hand under her cloak, resting on her lower back and pulling her closer to him, he first questioned, "Is my little she-wolf being curious?" He watched her nod before he captured her lips. He growled more when he felt her free arm move up his chest to rest at the back of his neck, bringing her even closer, as she opened to him. Although he knew she could feel how much he wanted her, and not just from his hardness, he used the way he was ravishing her lips to show her just how much he loved her. He was also very mindful of the people passing them by on the walkway. Forcing himself to end the kiss, Jim rested his head against hers as he let his breathing even out, feeling her breaths just as heavy. "Any questions?"

Brandi was more than just surprised by that kiss, she was floored. No one in her oh so very long life had EVER kissed her like that. "Oh my. That was ..." She said once her breathing had calmed. She quietly laughed because she couldn't even think of an appropriate word in English to finish her thought. Remembering he asked her something, she replied, "Nope. None whatsoever."

Jim rubbed his hand across her lower back, letting it slip slightly to move across her butt. Although he wanted more than to just have her as a bed partner, at the moment he was looking forward to when he was able to finally take her to bed and have her. Completely claim her as his. He kissed her once more before stepping to her side again. Resting his free hand back on hers, linking their fingers, he asked, "Did you just want to walk, or did you have a specific destination in mind, other than Alex's house?" Suddenly remembering something he'd forgotten to ask, he added, "Do you know if Alex has any staff at the house?"

"I don't think so. At least he didn't mention any when I asked him about staying there. Why?"

"The cart I just sent with our trunks. I asked the driver to remain until we arrive. I didn't want everything just left in the yard."

Brandi thought about it and nodded. "That makes sense. Hopefully it won't be too much of a problem for him. As for our walk, wherever we end up is fine. I just needed to be on solid land and not in a carriage or cart." She was just happy to be there with Jim. For a minute, she felt guilty at not having Lexi on her mind, but she shook that off just as quickly. She had spent the last year with no one but Lexi on her mind and she knew he wouldn't begrudge her being happy now, and he would be glad it was with Jim.

Jim's eyes shifted down to Brandi, wondering what she was thinking about. Giving her fingers a gentle squeeze, he smiled at seeing her eyes drift up to meet his. "Since the carriage didn't stop at noon and it's after four now, shall we find a restaurant?"

"Dinner sounds good."

Knowing her quietness, even with answering him, was unusual, he asked, "Penny for your thoughts?"

"Hmmm? Oh, sorry. Was just thinking about how Lex would be happy that I am here, with you. Even though he never asked, I think he suspected that you and I had more than just feelings of friendship toward each other. I believe he never asked because you and I never showed anything more than a close friendship and he knew I wouldn't ever have willingly cheated on him. I was also thinking about how nice it is to not just be here in London, but to be here with you."

Seeing a restaurant, Jim stopped, moving slightly to the side to let others go in and out. Like her brothers and stepdad, he tended to shorten her name when they were around others – since he knew most wouldn't understand him calling her Princess in public, and, until now, calling her baby in public wouldn't have been appropriate. "I'm glad to be here with you too, Bree. Thank you for asking me to join you." Unlinking their fingers, Jim lifted his hand from hers only to softly caress her face before he lightly brushed his lips across hers. He chuckled when he saw her bite her lip again. Noticing a drop of blood on her lower lip, he bent forward to take it in his mouth, effectively cleaning her lip. Moving his lips to her ear again, he said so only she would hear, "That is another thing I'm looking forward to. Feeling your fangs slide across my skin as well as penetrating it." Leaving her with that thought, he stepped to the door, opened it, and then followed her inside.

Dinner had been good – relaxing – although Jim's last comment kept floating through Brandi's mind. She wasn't sure how long she'd be able to stay with being courted. Stepping out of the restaurant, Brandi shivered, having forgotten how chilly it was. Taking Jim's arm again, she was glad for her cloak and her gloves, although she was wishing she was wearing an actual coat. She could feel his hand on hers through her gloves giving her a feeling of comfort. Brandi was only partially surprised the snow was coming down again. "If there are any carriages available, I'm ready to ride."

Jim was glad Brandi had first clarified that she was talking about a carriage since the last of her comment made him want to ask what she wanted to ride. Clearing his throat to cover a laugh, Jim wiped some snow off her face. The snow was starting to come down heavier. Pulling off his coat, Jim lifted her cloak to put it around her. Satisfied, he stepped to the edge of the walkway to hail a carriage.

Brandi was happy to be in the carriage as it headed to the home of her stepdad, Alex. Instead of watching the snow-covered London roads, she rested her head on Jim's shoulder and closed her eyes. Because they had been traveling, Brandi had made sure to maintain human form instead of shifting into her natural state which resembled energy and light. Due to the fact that she was the only one of her race to have this ability of shifting at will, it was how — along with a frequent supply of blood — she re-energized. As a result, she was exhausted and could not prevent herself from dozing off. Feeling Jim's arm slip around her back, and his hand resting on her hip, she slid her head down slightly to rest on his chest while her arm slid around the front of his waist, her hand resting on his opposite hip as she curled into him on the seat. Without realizing, or trying, she was asleep

Chapter 3

Jim hadn't been surprised that Brandi had remained asleep when the carriage stopped in front of the house. He was glad he saw the cart was parked in front as he was helped out, but he noticed it was empty. Wondering what was going on, but not wanting to have the carriage footman take the still sleeping Brandi from the inside of the carriage, Jim shook his head at the footman, stepping in front of the man, and gently lifted her into his arms, bringing her out. "I'm sorry. I know you are the one to assist us out, but the lady can become upset if she is awakened suddenly and there's less chance she'd awake if I lifted her out. If the driver can wait a moment, I'll return shortly to pay him." He was happy to see the footman nod. Turning, Jim headed toward the house, only to be surprised when the door was opened, by a well-built man with skin the color of caramel that was shade or two darker than Brandi's, as he strode up the walkway. When the man reached Jim, with Brandi, Jim noted the man was the same height he was. Not wanting to be rude by reading the man's mind, Jim said, "Good evening. May I ask who you are?"

The man smiled and, just in case the man looking at him were to read his mind, he kept his true thoughts hidden and acted as if he'd never seen the woman nor the man who carried her before.

The woman being carried matched the description the man was given of his new 'mistress'. He wasn't sure about the man carrying her, but decided the man was safe since he held her gently. "I am Andre. Mambo Jacqueline Stewart send me to look after Mistress Brandi. I wasn't told about you, though." What Andre failed to mention was that he wasn't contacted by traditional means, that Andre wasn't his real name, that Jacqueline was able to communicate with spirits and Haitian gods, and that he just happened to fall into one of those categories. He actually knew who Jim was from having been keeping an eye, in his own way, on Brandi for centuries. Even though he'd been told by someone else that was close to Brandi that now wasn't to be his time with Brandi, Andre still came to act as Brandi's servant and protector at Jacqueline's request.

Hearing who sent Andre, Jim knew the man was okay. He also knew Alex must have contacted his mother in Haiti, Brandi's Grandmaman, to say that Brandi was coming to London but forgot to mention Jim would be with her. Jacqueline sent one of her Haitians to act as Brandi's servant. Giving Andre a slight nod, Jim replied as they stepped into the hall, "I'm Jim and am someone very close to your new mistress. Jacqueline knows me, but I think Jac's son forgot to mention I'd be here, and staying, with her granddaughter. Since your new mistress is sleeping, I will say for us both, I am glad you are here. If you are the one that retrieved our trunks, I thank you for that, too. If you will show me where our chamber is so I can lay her down, we can talk after I finish up with the carriage and cart drivers."

Attempting to hide a grin, Andre only nodded and, taking Jim up the stairs to the first floor, showed Jim to the main bed chamber.

Jim settled Brandi on the large four poster bed after waiting for Andre to carefully remove what looked like an overly large sheet from off the pillows and bedspread, then quickly went back downstairs and outside to see to both drivers, deciding to give both extra for the time waited. When he stepped back into the hall, he shook his head. At the moment, the house reminded him of the 'country' house that was just outside of St. Petersburg. Although he wanted to take a look around the ground floor, Jim joined Andre in what looked to be the drawing room.

Seeing Jim step into the room, Andre gave an apologetic look as he said, "I am sorry everything is still covered, including the bed upstairs. I have just arrived myself today and was not sure how soon Mistress Brandi would be here. It was not until your trunks arrived that I found which bed chamber would suit her. I had only finished taking the trunks in when you arrived."

Jim brushed off the apology. "Don't worry about it. I'll help you with it." Jim did a quick look at the room and burst out laughing. Seeing Andre glance over in question, Jim said, "I get having all these rooms but it just seems a waste to me. You have this drawing room where a couple, or the lady of the house, can receive callers. There is, usually, the parlor where the family itself can gather to spend time together. Most seem to also have a study for the man of the house to discuss any business – and can also double as a library, if there isn't one, to read or have a bit of quiet time, though there may also be a library to store all the books if the family has a large book collection. Then there is the large dining room for the more formal dinner parties, besides the breakfast room for just the family to have their meals together. I know I already said it, but there is too much wasted space. It seems there could just be one main room, like the parlor, that is comfortable but can be used for "entertaining" anyone that is from the *ton* or is important in any other way, as well as just for family and close friends instead of having all those separate." Sighing, Jim looked around again. "Why don't we leave everything covered in here for now since I doubt we'll even use this room while we're here." What he kept to himself was that if it did get used, it wouldn't be to spend time with any company.

"If you sure, sir," Andre told him, happy to not have to worry about that room. From what he'd been told before he was sent here, he would be acting as house staff while Brandi was there, while also helping with whatever she needed and, if necessary, acting as a bodyguard. Although he spoke English very well, he tended to slip into a type of Haitian creole where he still spoke in English, but shortened sentences by cutting words out, as he'd done a few times with Jim already. He was glad the man hadn't corrected his speech. Because he was acting as if he were curious, already knowing the answer since he'd been keeping an eye on Brandi from where he normally resided, but making it seem as if he wasn't wanting to broach it with his 'mistress', Andre asked Jim, using the Haitian form of grandma for Jacqueline, "'Scuse me sir, but Mistress Brandi's grann asked me to be a bodyguard, too. Is there some problem I should know about?"

Leaving the drawing room, with Andre following behind, Jim headed toward the next room. Although he couldn't see the furniture very well under their coverings, from its appearance he took it to be the parlor. Hearing the question as he started to uncover a chair, Jim glanced at Andre.

Unsure how much the other man knew regarding Brandi's heritage, he erred on the side of caution and referred to her as though this was her first and only 'life'. "Brandi and her younger brother were forcibly taken from outside her home in Russia when she was 10 years old. During the six years she was being held against her will, she was continually molested. A few years after her return to her family and now married, she, her late husband and two of his siblings, were kidnapped and badly abused. The man is still at large, although hopefully, he is still in Russia."

Jim stopped for a minute to let the anger toward the bastard that had taken them abate. When he felt he could continue calmly, Jim said, "Brandi didn't make a big deal about leaving to come here. Her late husband's parents, as well as her dad – who is Jac's son - and I are the only ones who knew she was leaving and to where. The only other person that also knows she is here is my brother, and he is also one, like me, that would protect her with his life. If Jac asked you to be her bodyguard, she is making sure Brandi is very well protected, because I am sure Jac would have told you to protect Brandi with your life. If you have any questions about the man, it's best to come to me and ask without Brandi nearby. The man causes her stress and worry, as well as frightens her, and since she is here to relax and have a holiday, I want to keep that stress and worry to a bare minimum, if possible."

Andre thought about Jim's words and nodded as he uncovered furniture in the parlor. "Yes, sir. I talk to you if questions. Makes sense on why the Mambo want me as my mistress's bodyguard." Taking the last cover off, Andre took the one Jim was holding before following Jim to the dining room. After what Jim said in the drawing room, Andre wasn't surprised to see the man just shake his head and move to the breakfast room. It didn't take them long to uncover the table and chairs. Taking these coverings from Jim, Andre asked, "Do you want to wait for uncovering in the study?"

Nodding, Jim said, "Yeah. If I decide to use it, I'll uncover whatever I need to at that time." Making a quick decision, knowing Brandi would agree, Jim then said, "If you haven't taken a bed chamber where the house servants' chambers are, take whatever chamber on the first floor you would like. Now, if you'll excuse me, I'm going to get some sleep. We'll see you in the morning."

"Thank you, sir. I have work to finish but I will choose one before I finish my work to add those covers. Good night, sir."

Jim just gave a small inclination of his head before heading upstairs.

Chapter 4

Brandi slept soundly. She had remained asleep when Jim laid her down but she woke just a few minutes later when she shifted. She'd remained shifted until she sensed a familiar presence nearby, even if the person was not quite in the room, causing her to return to looking human. Rousing again, as she sometimes did when shifting back and forth, Brandi opened her eyes slightly to see Jim coming in.

Jim wasn't surprised to see Brandi's eyes ajar. Sitting next to her, he asked, "Waking up, baby? I came up to join you."

Brandi gave him a sleepy smile. "No, not really fully awake. I could sleep more. I think I woke up from shifting and you coming in. I want to change, though. Help me, please?"

Standing, Jim helped her to first sit and then stand. Reaching around her, he undid the high-waist bow behind her before he unlaced the back of the dress. Moving his hands to her shoulders, he slipped the sleeves down her arms before he watched the dress slide over her generous curves to pool on the floor. Sliding his hands back around her, he undid the buttons of her petticoat before he moved it over her shoulders to slide off of her and join her dress. He was very tempted to pull the shift she still wore off over her head, but instead stepped around her to pull the upper sheet, blanket, and bedspread down for her. Helping her to sit and then lay back down, surprised she hadn't been falling asleep standing up, Jim covered her before picking up her dress and petticoat and draping them over a chair. Going around to the other side of the bed, he undressed before pulling down the covers and sliding in. Jim was glad when Brandi curled up against him, resting her head just below his shoulder. His arms went around her, keeping her close as he fell into an easy sleep.

Brandi was asleep the moment her head made contact with Jim's chest. The dream, she knew it was more a dream than a vision since it wasn't a memory, started almost immediately.

She was walking alone down a deserted road that was forested on both sides even though she could feel the pack of wolves nearby. Because they were her pack, they just watched and followed out of sight in the forest to her right. Hearing and sensing a herd of horses coming down the road, but not expecting them, she jumped slightly and then stumbled over something as she moved off the road to stay out of their way.

When she'd started to stand, while making sure nothing was hurt, a voice asked if she was all right. She smiled when she felt his hand grab her to help her steady. Looking up at him, she gauged him to be around six foot seven inches tall. With the smile still in place, she said, "Thank you. I believe I am. Thank you for also stopping to check on me."

She watched him grin as he replied, "You're very welcome. My friends and I didn't mean to startle you. We ride down this road several times a day to the cottage of The Wise One and back to town. The road really isn't safe to be walking alone, even during the day. There are wolves out here."

She maintained her bright smile, even though she wanted to laugh. She knew of the wolves out there, she was one of them normally. "That cottage is where I'm heading," she told him. "It's my grandfather's house. And

I've seen some wolves back in the trees at times but they've never bothered me."

"You're lucky. They can be dangerous. I didn't realize the elder had children or grandchildren."

She bit the inside of her bottom lip to keep from laughing at his comment about the wolves. When he mentioned her grandfather, she nodded. "I try to come out every day to see him. His name is Wind Rider, and I'm Brandi."

The man smiled. "Pleasure to meet you, Brandi. I'm Jim. He's a lucky man to have a granddaughter who likes to visit him as often as you do."

Brandi dipped her head in acknowledgment. "Nice to meet you, Jim. I'd say I'm the lucky one to have him and be able to learn all he has to teach." She gave him another smile before she continued up the road. She wanted to shift, but didn't in case he was part of the wolf hunting gang she'd heard about. She was surprised to see him at her side when she heard, "Would you like me to give you a ride? You'll get there faster."

Stopping, Brandi thought about his offer. She guessed that if she said no, he'd follow her just to make sure nothing else happened to her. Glancing up at him, she said, "Sure, thanks. That's kind of you."

Brandi noticed the grin Jim was trying to hide as he slid backward slightly on the saddle. "Climb on in front of me," he told her, taking a foot out of the stirrup and leaning down to give her an arm to help her up. Once she was in place, she couldn't help but notice the way he put his arms around her as he retook the reins, making sure he was holding her snugly. She also was well aware of where he rested his hand on her thigh as they rode.

When they got to her grandfather's and she'd dismounted, with Jim's help, she got a proper look at the tunic he wore. She mentally kicked herself for not paying closer attention prior to accepting the ride from him. He was part of the wolf hunting gang called the Red Hoods.

Greeting her grandfather, she also explained, when the elder man asked, why she had accepted a lift from Jim. Then she shifted into her wolf form and went outside, to join the rest of her pack.

Sometime later, Brandi decided to take a break and headed over to the pond behind her grandfather's house. She'd stayed in her wolf form to keep the other wolves comfortable. Not knowing why, her head shot up and she sniffed the air, as a trickle of unease rippled her fur. Something was wrong. Growling, she ran swiftly back towards the rest of the pack.

Seeing the arrows flying she snarled, and turned to see where they were coming from. Not seeing Jim, but spotting the familiar jacket, she didn't think about what she was doing when she charged the gang member closest to her.

She clamped her jaws around the arm holding the bow, only to be shaken off. Working at being a distraction and to keep the man from shooting the rest of the wolves, she continued her attack. She howled, a vicious stabbing piercing her side as an unseen arrow felled her

After the arrow struck her, Brandi had been drifting in and out of consciousness. She remembered being picked up and hearing Jim's voice, but not really being able to focus on his words. The pain was intense, more intense than anything she'd felt before. Then it seemed to ease a little just before her head was lifted and she smelled the tea her grandfather always made when she was hurt. She drank because she knew if she didn't it would be poured down her throat by her grandfather. She sighed as the tea worked its way into her system. She couldn't quite tell what, but it seemed there was something different about this brew since it seemed to take effect more quickly than usual.

As the pain began to ease even more, she was able to focus a little better on the conversation between her grandfather and Jim. She didn't understand why Jim said he could feel her pain, why he mentioned not being able to read someone's mind, and more importantly, why he said she had a mate now. She didn't have long to think on it when she felt the arrow being withdrawn causing her to whimper slightly. At this point, thankfully, it was more uncomfortable than painful. She thought it strange when she felt it stop instead of the arrowhead ripping out of her and, curiously, it was as though the arrowhead just dissolved before she felt the rest of the shaft slide out. Even more peculiar, whatever it was that was new in the tea seemed to enfold her, starting at her wound.

Slowly, her eyes opened and she shifted back to being human. She was still dressed but her top was pulled up slightly. Looking across the bed, she smiled at Jim. Not sure how her voice would sound, or even if it would be in English, she said, "Thank you." Seeing Jim incline his head in acknowledgment, she swallowed, adding, "What was that you said about pain, and reading minds, and mates?"

She watched Jim looked over at Wind Rider. When the older man nodded, Jim said, "First, can you read minds?" Because she'd inclined her head to say she could, he smiled. "Try reading mine." She felt her eyes widen, which caused him to ask, "Can you?" Since she shook her head, he almost laughed.

She was surprised when he took out his knife. He held it above his hand, nicking it slightly. She could see he wanted to ask her a question as she suddenly grabbed her hand, stare at it, and then cradle it because it was hurting – yet there was no cut on her hand. Once his hand was healed, he asked her, "Better?"

"Yes, thank you." She was intrigued, yet oddly, not particularly shocked.

"You're welcome. That's what I meant with regards to pain and reading minds. I can't read your mind either and I could feel when you were hurt. What that means is ..."

Brandi had been studying her hand but looked up at him as he was starting to explain. Biting her lip, she finished for him, "... is that we're mates?" Seeing him nod, she smiled, warmth flickering through her. "I think I can handle that. But how did you heal me?"

After having Jim tell her how he'd healed her, she then found out all about him. In his telling, he included about his race, how old he was, and that he could also shift. When he was done, Brandi found herself sharing about herself with him too.*

Jim was asleep as quickly as Brandi had been. Without knowing it, when he started dreaming, his dream mirrored Brandi's although where hers went dark for a short time, his showed the dream version of himself talking to his second-in-charge and then returning to remove the arrow from her side. In his conscious state, he had no idea why he would be dreaming about being the leader of some wolf hunter gang and having the dream include Wind Rider. When the dream just seemed to end, he did wish he could see more of their life together, but, as he felt the real woman he was holding onto start to move in closer, he started to wake – in more ways than one.

Chapter 5

Starting to wake from her very strange dream, Brandi curled into Jim more causing her to be nearly lying on top of him. Sliding a hand across his chest, her leg moved from where it had been, resting with her knee at the level of his hips and her foot draped across his knee to her knee sliding across his hips with her leg following. When her knee stopped against something stiff, she slid her hand from his chest, down across his abdomen. Finding what she sought, her hand closed around his hardness. As it did, she both heard and felt him take in a quick breath. Opening her eyes, Brandi smiled when she saw he was gazing at her. Positioning herself so she was straddling his leg – appearing as if she was riding his thigh - she only asked, "Please?"

Jim didn't need any further encouragement. He could feel his thigh getting wet from her arousal as he got harder from her stroking. Lifting her off his thigh, he fisted the hem of her shift in his hands, dragging it up over her hips. Pulling her to him, his lips took and ravaged hers while his fingers found their target and started their own onslaught. Feeling her hand suddenly stop stroking, he started to growl until he felt her bucking on his fingers, trying to move her body to take them into her. Moving his hands back to her hips, he lifted her up, guiding her onto him, breaking their kiss to grind out, "I have so much more I plan on doing, but I need to fuck you. Now."

Brandi didn't plan on arguing. She wanted him in her, pounding her, making her cry out his name. The moment he was fully sheathed in her, she started moving on him, riding him. Almost immediately, she exploded around him, screaming her pleasure. She could feel his hands on her hips, though, in some coherent part of her mind, she wasn't sure if he was only resting them there or helping her move. Wanting him to see all of her, Brandi drew her shift up over her head, throwing it off to the side. She felt an immense satisfaction when she heard his rumble of appreciation as his hands strayed up her abdomen to her breasts, cupping them, each thumb chaffing over her nipples.

Jim couldn't keep a coherent thought in his head, yet he could intensely feel all her pleasure on top of his own. He could feel how nice and tightly she hugged him while giving and expanding as was needed. He never thought he could fill her this easily and fully, yet she took him all in without a problem as though she had been created just for him. As vigorously as he was pounding her, she met him thrust for thrust with a wild abandon. Sitting up, his mouth and teeth replaced a thumb on one breast as he felt her legs wrap around him, moving harder and faster on him as if trying to draw him in deeper. As she kept riding and soaking him with her continuous release, a scent that for some reason seemed familiar to him despite never having come across it before - the mating scent and, for them, was the combination of his tiger and her wolf – permeated the air. Jim knew Brandi's animal of choice for shifting was a wolf, even though she was able to become any animal she chose. His tiger wanted to fully claim her as his mate as much as Jim did, but before he had the chance to say anything, Jim felt her hands tug his head from her breast. Meeting her eyes, which had changed to look like those of a wolf, he wasn't surprised to hear her demand, "Please ... now ... claim me." Not needing to be asked twice, his mouth transformed into that of his tiger and his now strong jaw clamped down between her shoulder and her neck as he gave one last powerful thrust, feeling her legs tighten slightly like she knew what was coming, and emptied into her. He felt her final release as she pulsed around him, as though she was trying to get every last drop just before he felt the shape of her mouth shift against his neck, and her fangs pierced his skin so she could drink. Making sure he didn't rip her skin off, Jim lifted his head, letting his mouth revert to normal, smiling at Brandi when he felt her move slightly and then spasm, soaking him more with an aftershock. Holding her close, he turned so they were lying on their side with her being more under him now.

Brandi sighed with contentment as she ran her hands along Jim's back. Even if Jim had called it a fucking, she knew it was more than that. Not in a very long time had someone given himself to her and her to him as she and Jim just had. She also had never wanted to be claimed, although to her knowledge she'd never had someone that wanted to claim her, by anyone as she had wanted Jim to claim her. Nor had she ever wanted to claim another as she had wanted to claim him – her mind went to Lexi briefly, giving her a stab of guilt, not just at the fact she was lying naked under Jim, but because she'd never wanted to lay any kind of claim on Lexi.

As quick as the guilty feeling had come, it was gone – it was like she'd heard Lexi tell her it was all right, the visions she had could change or shift and she was where she needed to be. She shook off the feeling since it was gone, but she thought about the vision he'd mentioned, one that she'd had earlier in their marriage about someone she'd never seen prior but she saw a future with that man well into what looked like the future. Letting the vision go, she refocused on Jim and how much she loved him – as well as how long she'd loved him.

Her claim on Jim had been two-fold – her wolf – which would go over to any other animal she shifted into - and the vampire, although the vampire in her drank from him for nourishment as well as the healing properties of his blood. Gazing up at him, she softly smiled. "Although I don't think either of us could go another round yet, if that was just fucking me, I can't wait to see what making love to me will be like." Feeling safe wrapped in his arms, Brandi gave a small yawn and then said, "I had the strangest dream." She frowned slightly when Jim suddenly sat up, resting on his elbow to look at her in astonishment.

Jim felt something from her he couldn't quite put a name on and, before he'd had the chance to figure it out and ask her, it was gone. Feeling her relax again, he let whatever it was he'd felt from her go – at least for the moment. Instead, he found himself chuckling at her comments – of not being able to do a second round and at wondering what making love to him will be like. He wasn't surprised at the yawn since he was ready for some sleep again. He wasn't ready for her last comment. "I did too. In what way was your dream strange? Will you tell me about it?"

Wondering about his dream too, Brandi only nodded. She then proceeded to tell him all about the dream only to find her mouth falling open as he easily picked up where she left off, filling in areas that had been blank for her, or she was just unaware of, since it had been what he had been seeing and going through. Finding one thing strange, she asked, "Could you figure out why you were the leader of a gang of wolf hunters called the Red Hoods?"

Jim shook his head. "I have no idea, baby. That was the one thing I couldn't figure out. We both do know it wasn't any kind of a memory, and I seriously doubt it was a vision of the future since we are much older than we were in the dream." Leaning down he gave her a kiss filled with love, though it was gentler than the bruising one he'd given her not long ago, then laid down next to her, pulling her back close so her head was once again resting on his shoulder. "For now, let's get some more sleep. I'm glad you drank some since I know you hadn't in the last month, like you hadn't shifted, even though you've needed both. If you shift again while we sleep, and don't wake until morning, it's fine. You probably need that restoration. Oh, by the way, Alex must have told Jac you were coming to London. She sent you a Haitian to have as a house servant and bodyguard. His name is Andre and he seems nice enough."

Feeling herself fall asleep, Brandi heard Jim, but only managed to nod in response before she was fully asleep. Even though this time she didn't wake, she shifted to looking like light and energy shortly thereafter.

Glad to see she shifted, Jim drifted off within a minute or two after Brandi, feeling content and satisfied.

Chapter 6

Brandi met Andre the next morning. Since the man was sent by her grann, she wasn't surprised he was Haitian. She also wasn't surprised at how built he was. She found it amusing that when they were at home, he was rarely seen – which made it very easy for Jim and Brandi to enjoy each other in most of the ground floor rooms, as well as going out behind the house – both shifting into a white tiger – since Jim was also a white tiger, she shifted into the same instead of her preferred wolf - and enjoying. They couldn't seem to get enough of each other now that they'd finally taken that step.

Through Andre making some discreet inquiries, Brandi found out what parties were being put on by members of the *ton*. For any that were by invitation only, having the name of each woman holding the party, she wrote each hostess a brief note to explain who she was and that she was in London for the rest of the season, adding a request to call on the woman in question. Brandi was surprised when she'd received a reply, over the first week in London, from each with an acceptance for her to call on them and telling her when would be the best time. She was glad that none were at the same time.

Watching Brandi that first week, Jim couldn't help but smile. He knew she would disagree, since he had yet to see her host or attend a party in St Petersburg, but she looked in her element. It was a life he wanted to give her, knowing he'd be able to do just that without a problem. Alex had given him the money for their traveling as well as enough for spending –

which included any wardrobe Brandi needed. Jim still had every penny Alex gave him. Before they'd left, after she'd asked him to join her, Jim made sure to get more than enough for the trip, knowing he could find a bank in London to withdraw more if needed. What he hadn't expected was to run into Ken. Ken had said to notify him if Jim ran low on money. When Jim asked him why he needed to do that, that he could make a withdrawal, Ken reminded him that the Bank of England may not give Jim money since technically the bank Jim used was in Russia. Jim had told Ken he'd let him know if it was needed. Chuckling to himself, Jim wouldn't be surprised if Ken suddenly decided he needed to be in London.

Hearing Jim, Brandi looked up from the missive she was answering. "What's funny?"

Stepping to her, Jim ran his hand down her hair as he grinned. "A stupid thought that made me laugh." Seeing her raised eyebrow, the grin deepened as he shook his head. "You may not be able to read my mind, baby, but you do know me well. I was just thinking that I wouldn't be surprised if Ken decides to show up in London."

Brandi stood, rising on her toes to give him a kiss. Ending the kiss on a sigh, she asked, "Does he have a reason to, other than coming to lend you money temporarily?"

Jim pulled Brandi closer, dipping down to nuzzle her neck. Lifting back up, he shook his head. "Since, obviously, you were listening to us, no. That would be the only reason. And only if I let him know. Also, before you ask, I don't foresee having to borrow from him. It would only be if I can't make a withdrawal from the bank. Also, I have separate money Alex gave me for the trip and for anything for you. What I didn't tell Alex was I already had the trip taken care of and planned on getting anything you needed myself, and that would have been even if our relationship hadn't recently changed – for the better. Speaking of getting you anything you need, shall we make a trip and see what they have available now and order what isn't?"

Brandi bit her lip, trying not to giggle. "You are actually volunteering to go shopping with me? I just need to get my reticule, as well as my hat, and I'll be ready. How do you plan on us getting to any shops?"

"Yeah, surprisingly, I am volunteering." Tipping her face up so he would be looking her in the eyes, he gave a hint of a smile. "Let's just say it's because I love you. I had Andre rent us a carriage and horses to use for the time we're here. He'll be our carriage driver. That way, when you are out by yourself, he'll always be near, even if I'm not."

Brandi sighed at his reason for going with her as she looked up into his eyes. Anytime she did, she found herself getting lost in their depths. Giving him a soft smile, she said, "I love you too." Thinking about the rest of what he said, she nodded. "That makes sense for renting and I'm glad he will be. Thank you."

The hint of a smile he'd had turned into a full smile as he acknowledged her words. "Shall we grab your bag and hat and go, then?"

Riding in the carriage the next day, Brandi let her mind drift back to the shopping trip. Even though she rarely went shopping, Brandi knew what the prices of dresses, shifts, and petticoats were for what they were looking at – in the price range only those of the higher end of the *ton* could afford. She wasn't worried about Jim not being able to afford it. She knew, like her stepdad, Alex, as well as herself, Jim could more than afford what they were looking at for her daily and evening wardrobe. The part Brandi was surprised about was that they managed to go to shops where a modiste & her seamstresses worked. Brandi chose the styles, colors, and materials she wanted for the dresses – day wear, evening wear, and riding habits - as well as giving the house address so all her purchases could be delivered. In each shop, the modiste asked which dress she'd wanted immediately because the woman, along with her seamstresses, would get that one done by the end of the evening to deliver to her. Since she hadn't needed any of the evening ones yet, at three of the shops she made her choice of which single dress she desired. She loved the various styles she'd chosen, in all her favorite colors. Brandi had also been amazed at how well Jim knew her taste in clothing – and how fast he'd figured it out. She'd decided to wear one of the new dresses that had been delivered the evening before - a soft peach color. Smoothing out the skirt, she grinned to herself at how well the color of this gown complimented her skin tone. She didn't know why she was surprised at that, since it was a color Jim picked out for her. Feeling the carriage stop, she slid to be closer to the door before giving Andre a smile and then placing her hand in his as he helped her out.

Brandi nearly bounced as Jim assisted her into the carriage, after he made sure the stallion's reins were tied securely to the back. She was glad he rode to the club, using one of the riding horses Andre had found for them to use, and that he had spent the day at the club while she made the day's rounds for calling on the different ladies of the *ton* that she made appointments to visit today. Since he knew who her last visit of the day was with, he made a point to ride back with the husband of the woman she'd just been to see. It was nice to have him riding home with her. Leaning against him in the shadows of the interior, Brandi quietly sighed in contentment before turning her gaze up to him. "Thank you."

Jim pulled her close as he chuckled. "Of course, baby. I did promise to court you properly and I still plan to do that. Besides, do you really think I'd turn down the chance to take a slow carriage ride with a beautiful woman who also happens to be my favorite girl?"

"Slow carriage ride?" Slightly sitting up, Brandi looked across Jim and out the window. Not recognizing where they were, she looked at Jim questioningly.

Jim chuckled more at the look on her face. Leaning down, he kissed her gently. "Yeah. I asked Andre to take a detour. I thought you might enjoy a ride through the park and then dinner at the restaurant we ate at the first day here."

Brandi grinned. "That sounds fantastic. Thank you again. You are the best."

Jim had switched positions with Brandi on the seat, so it was easier for her to look out the window as they drove through the park. The look of pure joy on her face had him forgetting she was 41 years old, since who he saw was the girl he'd fallen in love with so very long ago.

He enjoyed riding through the park himself – the weak light dappling on the snow covered ground through the beautiful white trees as the sun was going down, the woman he loved – his mate – at his side, couples – looking like they were in love – strolling along the walkway through the cold and blanketed park. If this was courting a woman, he admitted to himself he had never courted a woman since he had only ever wanted one, he was all for it and would continue to do this as long as he could and as often as he could.

Chapter 7

February 1805

Brandi smiled at Andre as the Haitian removed her and Jim's breakfast plates. She was surprised it was already February. The month in London seemed to just fly by, although she wasn't anywhere near ready to return to Russia. She missed her family, which included Dominique and Dominique's husband Dmitri, but she had messaged her brothers Mike and Eric to send her wolves to her. She hadn't been surprised when they showed up with her two boys, bringing along a very familiar third wolf. She was brought out of her thoughts when she felt a head rest on her leg. Looking down briefly, she absently rubbed the head of Hercules, the smaller of her two wolves. Biting her lip, she had been glad her cousin Grayson had come with her brothers, but she made sure their visit was short and not overnight. It wasn't that she hadn't wanted them to stay, she had just wanted them to go.

Leaning back in his chair, Jim rubbed the head of Ares, Brandi's other wolf, without thinking about it as he gazed at Brandi. "Penny for your thoughts, baby?"

Brandi focused on Jim, her smile growing. "I'm glad Mike and Eric brought these two, even if Gray tagged along, but I'm even happier that all three took the hint and didn't stay. I'm not ready to go back, but I've loved the month here. I'm tempted to send for Anna and stay here for an extended time."

"We can stay as long as you want. As for Anna, all you can do is ask her, baby. She's an adult and has her life there." After giving Ares a final pat, Jim stood and stepped to Brandi's side. Leaning over, he kissed the top of her head. "What do you have planned for the day?"

Brandi knew he was right about Anna and that she could only ask Anna if she wanted to come to London. Brandi was glad they didn't have to hurry up to go back to Russia, also. London was feeling more like home at the moment. At his question, Brandi rolled her eyes. "Lunch with Virginia and planning for some ball or whatnot that she plans to hold a week from tomorrow. Valentine themed, I believe, but since Valentine's Day is during the week, she wants to hold it the weekend before. In my opinion, it's just a frivolous reason to hold another damn ball."

Jim burst out laughing. "Here I thought you enjoyed all the parties we've gone to." Not recognizing the other woman's name, he asked, "Virginia?"

Brandi nodded. "Jack Thompson's wife." Seeing recognition dawn on his face, Brandi giggled. "As to the balls, yes, but only because I have been at them with you and I wasn't part of the planning before. We may technically be part of the *ton*, but you know I'm more comfortable in the country with a stable of horses and not having to attend so many useless parties. What about you? What do you have planned today?"

Bending over, Jim lifted Brandi off the chair only to sit down and then put her on his lap. "I have a couple appointments and no, I'm not going to tell you what about. You'll find out soon enough." Jim had made appointments with a goldsmith and a jeweler to see about having a couple of rings made. He hoped that they would be able to do what he wanted and have them ready in just about two weeks. He had big plans, snow or not, for her for Valentine's Day. In public, he did as she'd first asked when they'd arrived in London, he properly courted her – they went to any of the balls she finagled an invitation to and he made sure to let all men know that she wasn't looking for anyone, she was already taken. In private, it was a whole different matter - whether it was during the day, on the off chance neither had a reason for going out, when they both happened to be home, or at night – they showed each other how much they loved each other. Despite knowing they couldn't avoid socializing, Jim preferred it being just the two of them. Even though he had spent most of the very many years they'd known each other away from her, he could admit he loved any of time he'd spent with her, after Dominique had sent him a message as to where to be able to find her, over the last 26 years.

Resting his head against hers, he mentally shook off his thoughts. Returning his gaze to her, he found her staring at him. "Sorry, mind wandered. I'm still not telling you, baby." He stood, easily keeping her in his arms, and then carried her upstairs. Jim helped Brandi with what she needed for her hooking the back of her petticoat and then doing the laces on her dress before he changed his own clothes.

Brandi watched from the carriage window as Jim headed off on horseback. He looked to be going toward Bond Street. She knew he helped Andre with some of the purchases for the house, but they hadn't mentioned needing any supplies lately, so she wondered why he was going that way. He did mention having a couple appointments and that she would be finding out what they were about. Deciding it was better to leave it, and not ask Andre if he knew what it was about, she sat back for the rest of her ride.

As he rode from the house, Jim quietly laughed. He didn't need to feel what she did to know she wanted to know what he was up to. Reaching Bond Street, he found the address for the goldsmith and jeweler he was to meet – Stedman & Vardon were their names.

Jim's appointments went well. He had them making two rings for him, one that he would give Brandi when he asked an important question, if she answered that question the way he was hoping, and the other to give her later. Jim was glad they could have the main ring done by when he'd requested. He made an appointment with them to pick it up on Valentine's Day. It was a day he was looking forward to.

Chapter 8

Valentine's Day

Brandi sat at the dressing table Jim had made for her, getting ready for ... well, she wasn't exactly sure what for. All she knew was Jim told her he was taking her out for a special evening. Then she'd found a card on the dressing table that he'd made telling her what time she needed to be ready by and that she should wear one of her best gowns. She looked at the card she'd made for him, not having the chance to give it to him yet since she hadn't seen him all day. Stopping midway through brushing her hair, she let her mind drift briefly over the last couple weeks. To her surprise, the ball had gone off without a hitch and everyone seemed to enjoy it. Returning to her hair, she finished getting ready.

Jim stood at the door, just watching Brandi. He could see her mind was elsewhere, since she hadn't realized he was standing there yet. Seeing her finishing up, he cleared his throat and smiled when she turned her gaze to him, looking surprised. "It's rare I can actually surprise you. You ready to go, baby?"

Grabbing the card as well as her hat, gloves and reticule, she nodded then stood, returning the smile. "Are you going to tell me what you've got planned now?" Seeing him shake his head, she gave him a mock sigh as she rolled her eyes. Stopping at the door, she handed him his card then stood on her toes to lightly kiss him, only to move quickly away before he could grab her. Giggling as she went downstairs, she called back up, "If we're going, shouldn't we be on our way?" Reaching the bottom, she took her cloak from Andre. "Thank you."

"You're welcome, mistress."

Jim got to the bottom of the stairs and also took his coat from Andre. Taking Brandi's hand, he asked, "Shall we?"

It didn't take them long to reach their destination. Getting out of the carriage, Jim helped Brandi down. Seeing the look of disbelief on her face, he chuckled knowing he'd surprised her a second time that night. Tucking her arm in his, he had them following Andre down the snow-covered walkway.

"The park?" She asked in wonderment. "Isn't it a bit cold to be here in the evening?"

Jim stopped when Andre did and then waited until Andre had everything set up and had moved away. "Yeah, it is cold, but, although I didn't want to be at home, I still wanted it to just be us and not around a room filled with people." Letting go of her arm, he pulled a small box out of his pocket and then said, "I have one thing I want to do, well more like ask, before we sit to enjoy this dinner Andre cooked for us." Taking her left hand, he sunk down to one knee. "I love you, Brandi, and have loved you for more years than I care to think about. Would you do me the honor of marrying me and being my wife?"

Brandi was speechless as a tear slid down her face. This was the last thing she had expected from him. Dropping to her own knees, she suddenly kissed him before hugging him close. Leaning back, she gave him a radiant smile and, as she nodded, she said, "Yes. A thousand times yes. Nothing would make me happier than to be your wife."

Chapter 9

February 1805

Jim asking her to marry him surprised her. During the moment or two she'd been speechless she'd had a sense of guilt, as she occasionally had since they'd first arrived in London and changed the way their relationship was, the feeling of cheating on her late husband Lexi but just as quick as the guilt came it was gone along with hearing Lexi's voice in her ear quietly telling her he approved. The next day, after spending half the morning in bed with Jim, Brandi wrote letters to her stepdad Alex, as well as her brothers and daughter in Russia, and her grandparents in Haiti to let them know she and Jim were getting married and they'd decided on Valentine's Day the next year to have the wedding. With how late in the morning it was, she had known the letters wouldn't go out until the next day and that there wouldn't be any reply – at least via mail – for at least a month. The rest of that day Brandi spent at home making lists with Jim of what all they would need to do, together and separately, for the wedding. She was glad for the friends she'd made, as well as the balls they'd gone to, so she knew who to contact with regards to food.

It hadn't surprised her when Jim asked, "Did you want my help with deciding on your dress?" Brandi had laughed and then shook her head before she told him, "Thanks, but no. I want you to be surprised."

After Jim left and before she and Andre left to head to the shops, Brandi sat down with her sketch pad and drew what she wanted for a wedding dress – high waist - slightly more fitted than her regular evening gowns - with a scoop neck and long sleeves, closer fitted at the wrists and putting lace for the sleeves from the upper arm down – adding that to the notes for it being what she wanted, and short train in back - as well as putting notes to the side for the color she wanted the dress. With the sketch in hand, she returned to one of the shops that she had purchased some of the rest of her wardrobe and talked to the modiste & her seamstresses about needing a wedding dress. When she was asked what she wanted, she handed the woman the sketch and said, "This is what I would like. I added what notes I thought you may need onto it."

The modiste took the paper from Brandi, looked it over and nodded. "This is perfect. Thank you very much. When will the wedding be held?"

Smiling, Brandi was glad there wasn't a problem with her drawing what she wanted. "You're welcome. It won't be until Valentine's Day next year."

"That's good. It gives us plenty of time. I have your measurements so we will get started on this. I will let you know when it is time for your first fitting."

When letters arrived from Russia and Haiti, both Brandi and Jim were happy that everyone had replied that they would be there, as well as Alex saying that he didn't mind them holding the wedding at the house. Jim also let her know he'd heard from both Ken and Brian and they would also be attending.

Looking through the mail, Jim did a quick count. "Including both of my brothers, and it looks like Anna contacted Will to let Leah know – and Leah, at least, will be able to come, so we'll have fourteen – fifteen if it's in the evening after Will wakes up. I didn't see Alex mention Devlin or Wind Rider. Did you let them both know and have either gotten back to you if you did?"

Brandi glanced over her shoulder at him and smiled. "Actually, I did let them both know, but no, I haven't received any message yet. I'm not sure how they'll let me know if they do, or if they'll just decide to show up. They may have let Alex know but want it to be a surprise." Realizing she'd called one of her dad's by his name when Jim came around and raised an eyebrow at her, Brandi only shrugged as she giggled. "I probably called him Alex as to not confuse you as to which dad I was talking about. I also let Poppa Quinn, know, but I haven't heard anything from him. I am curious though. Shall I send out invitation missives to the few friends we have here in town, also?"

Jim thought about it for a moment. "I want to say yes, but did you fully read any of the replies, specifically the one from Jac, or did you just scan to see if they would make it?"

Brandi looked chagrined. "I scanned more to see if they were a yes or no. Why? What'd I miss?"

Jim handed her the letter from her grann and only said, "Read."

Taking it, Brandi read:

Pitit pitit fi (Granddaughter),

Thank you for inviting us to your wedding to Jim. You know your Granpè and I wouldn't want to miss it for anything. There is just one thing. By the time you receive this letter, we will be on a ship to America. We are moving to New Orleans, Louisiana, where your uncle, Ben, will be building us a large and lovely home.

You didn't mention where you planned on holding the wedding, so there is something we would like to ask - give you an option. Would you consider traveling to America to be married at our home? You could then spend your honeymoon here with us as well as explore New Orleans. I do understand that it means you would only be able to invite our family as well as Jim's, but we would love to share this with you both by having the wedding here. Unfortunately, you would also need to push the wedding back from next February to at least next March.

As soon as we arrive, I will let you know of an address to respond to with your answer.

With much love,

Grann

Getting to the end, she looked back up at Jim. "I guess I should have fully read it. I know it would mean letting the rest of the family know it won't be here and it will be in March of next year, but ... should we?"

"I'm fine with it, baby. It sounds like a great idea – give us a chance to see America now since it's been several millennia since we were last there and that was well before the British or anyone else settled there. I also think that was nice of her to ask and offer. The only thing I would want to do, before you send new letters out or message those you can't send letters too, is to message Ken to see if he would be able to take us over as well as work out the details with him for the trip."

Glancing back at the letter, she raised her gaze to Jim and gave a small nod. "Why don't you go ahead and message Ken then, and work out the details for the trip. I have a feeling he'll say it's fine. I'll get a letter written up to Grann to tell her thank you and we'll be happy to accept her offer so once she lets me know where to send a new letter too, I'll be able to mail it. I won't notify anyone else until after you've talked to Ken and I've mailed the new letter to Grann." Brandi suddenly giggled. "I wonder what that area is like in the Spring."

Chapter 10

February 2nd, 1806

Looking at the packed trunks in the entrance hall, Brandi smiled. She couldn't believe they were leaving for America the next day and getting married in just over a month. She was happy, happier than she'd been in a very long time – in at least 4,700 years. Brandi also realized that she hadn't felt any guilt like she was cheating on Lexi – or at least his memory – from being with Jim in several months. Her dress was carefully, but well packed - and where Jim wouldn't accidentally see it. Brandi was thankful the modiste and the modiste's seamstresses had been able to finish it earlier than planned – including doing Brandi's fittings.

When the letter from her grann arrived, once her grandparents were in America, Brandi immediately wrote back to say they were happy to move the date of the wedding to March and hold it in New Orleans. Brandi let her grann know what they wanted with regards to food. She also added that she had her dress already. She had finished the letter saying she would leave the preparations in her grann's hands though if Grann had any questions, to let her know.

"Everything ready, baby?" Jim had been standing on the stairs a few steps up from the bottom, watching Brandi for a few minutes before he'd asked his question.

Brandi jumped slightly at hearing Jim's voice. She was so lost in thought she hadn't realized he was there. Turning, she smiled up at him. "As ready as can be." She looked chagrined as she added, "I'm glad Grann offered, even with us having to travel there. She can worry about all of the preparations with the exception of my dress, which I packed well enough so no one will see it before the wedding. I will see if she needs any help once we're there." Moving around a trunk toward the stairs and Jim, Brandi finally asked, "Are these going to be sitting here until we leave tomorrow?"

Descending the rest of the way, Jim reached her first. Chuckling, he put his arms around her. "Actually, no. Ken rented a cart and is on his way over. He is bringing Brian with him too. The three of us are going to take the trunks down to the port and onto Ken's ship. What about Andre?"

"His is the one off to the side there. I'm not sure if he needs anything from it on the ship. For ours, the two bottom ones don't have anything we need until we get to Grann and Granpè's and can be stored for the trip if needed. This one on top we will need in whatever cabin Ken gives us."

Hearing the door open, Jim looked up and smiled at his brothers as the two men walked in. "Perfect timing. I just need to see where Andre wants his trunk. While I do that, these three can go out. This top one is for whatever cabin we're in, the other two can go into cargo." Starting to leave, after giving Brandi a kiss, Jim suddenly stopped. Thinking of something, he looked at Ken and asked, "Is it just us or are you taking any other cargo?"

Stepping to the trunks, Ken shook his head. "Just you three besides me, Brian and my crew. When you asked if I would take you to America and where you planned on going, I made some inquiries to see if there was a port in New Orleans I could sail into. When I was told there was, I've spent the last several months doing what I needed to for merchant trips so I wouldn't have to take any other cargo." Ken picked up the top trunk to carry it out to the waiting cart as Brian picked up a trunk to follow Ken out.

Jim quietly chuckled as he again turned to go find Andre only to be stopped short again as Andre joined them.

"Just the man I was looking for," Jim said to the Haitian. "Did you want your trunk in your cabin on the ship?"

Andre nodded. "Yes, if no trouble." Picking up his own trunk, Andre headed outside with it.

Between the four men, the trunks were loaded on the cart quickly. Following Andre back in the house, Jim found Brandi covering furniture in the parlor. Moving to her, he leaned down to kiss her before saying, "I'll be back soon, baby. Andre will be here. Shouldn't take us long to get the ship loaded."

Even though Ken apologized, Brandi still had some reservations about him, like he was still holding back for blaming her. Glad that Jim couldn't read her mind since she didn't want to upset him if he fully believed his brother, Brandi nodded. Knowing, no matter her feelings, she still needed to be somewhat polite, she said, "All right. Also, let them both know they can stay here in the house for the night if they don't want to spend it on the ship, please."

Jim could see her offer was half-hearted and, even though they hadn't talked about it, he could sense her distrust of Ken still. He couldn't blame her and fully understood. He wasn't quite sure his brother was on the up and up for the apology. Knowing it wasn't the time or place to talk about it, Jim smiled at her. "I'll let them know." Holding her close before giving her one more kiss, Jim headed out.

February 3rd, 1806

Brandi was excited as she finished getting ready to leave. They were finally leaving for America and for New Orleans where her grandparents lived. For the most part, she was glad Ken and Brian had returned with Jim to stay in the house overnight instead of on the ship. She was happy the three had taken the trunks over the day before making it one less thing they needed to worry about.

Jim stepped into the room. "Ready, baby?"

Smiling at him through the mirror, she nodded just before she put on her hat. "Just need to put my gloves on and grab my reticule." Standing, she pulled on the gloves that had been sitting next to her.

Stepping to her, Jim pulled Brandi close as he leaned down to kiss her. "Shall we?" He wondered after ending the kiss. Glad to see her nod, he continued with, as they headed downstairs, "I know you said you'd see if Jac needs help with the final preparations, but are you, yourself – not any of the extra details that may be left – ready to marry me?"

Brandi stopped just before they reached the bottom of the stairs and turned to look up at Jim. "I do believe I have been ready to be your wife longer than I have ever realized. You are my best friend and the man I have loved for the majority of my life. You are only one of two people that I have told everything about myself, well you've known from pretty much having always been there, and the other one died roughly 4,700 years ago. It may have taken us a long time to get here, but being with you as your wife is where I want to be." Moving up a step so she was even with him, Brandi put her arms around him to kiss him, showing Jim just how much she loved him and was ready for this next step.

Finishing the kiss, Jim dipped his head to nuzzle her neck. Quietly chuckling, Jim said in her ear, "If we weren't leaving in the next five minutes I'd carry you back upstairs to show me more of that." Placing a gentle kiss where he'd just been nuzzling, he added, "Since I know I haven't told you recently, Bree, I love you."

Brandi giggled at his comment and then sighed at the lightly placed kiss. "I love you too, Jim." Thinking of something else, Brandi softly asked, "Is it bad that I haven't thought of Lexi in months and that I no longer feel guilty?"

Jim shook his head. "No, it isn't bad. It just shows you've moved past grieving his loss. Since you aren't feeling guilty anymore over what we have, you haven't had a reason to think about him. It doesn't mean you won't think about him at times, especially since I'm sure that if there isn't one already there, soon there will be a ghost in residence at Dominique and Dmitri's house. I am also sure that same ghost will be keeping an eye on Anna."

Brandi thought about it. Before she had a chance to answer, Brandi heard a throat clear in the front lobby. Looking over Jim's shoulder, she smiled. "We're ready, Bri. We had just stopped to talk for a moment." Giving her attention back to Jim, and slipping her hand into his outstretched one, she said, "That makes sense as to why I'm not. I also think you're correct with regards to the ghost."

The trip to the port was both quiet and short. Ken had them wait to board, though Brian went ahead and boarded, until after Andre returned from leaving the two horses and carriage at the livery near the port where he'd already left the few horses from the house to be taken care of while they were gone.

Brandi was a bit surprised that Ken and Brian had waited to ride with them instead of leaving earlier that morning to return to the port to make sure the ship was ready to sail. She was more surprised when they got on board and Ken showed her and Jim to his cabin again. Stopping Ken before he moved away, Brandi asked, "Are you sure, Ken? You don't need to give us your cabin again."

Ken couldn't help but smile. "I know I don't have to, Princess. But I want to. Brian and the rest of my crew is aware I won't be in it so they won't mistakenly come in thinking I'm in there. I really don't mind." Leaning down, Ken kissed her cheek. "I'm sure you have questions about the trip. I'll be back as soon as I show Andre to his cabin."

Raising her eyebrow as if she was daring him to admit he'd read her mind, Brandi only gave Ken a quick nod before following Jim into their cabin.

Brandi stood at the rail just watching the water. A smile lit her features as she thought about some dolphins she had glimpsed swimming alongside the ship earlier. She stayed out of the way of Ken and his crew whenever she was on deck. And if Ken, Brian (when Brian was on deck), or Jim told her to immediately get below deck, she didn't argue, but that had only happened once in the almost two weeks they'd been sailing. Even though she knew the storm they'd sailed through had caused her to remain in the cabin and had done what Ken told her could happen – lengthen the trip – Brandi still looked out at the horizon in hopes of seeing land. Before they'd left Ken told her and Jim, though she guessed Jim was already well aware, that the trip across the Atlantic could be anywhere from two weeks to a month. When she asked him why it could take longer, he'd said that it would depend on the weather and any storms they possibly came across.

"Penny for your thoughts?" Jim asked. He liked it when he could come upon her unawares.

Brandi giggled and leaned back. She knew he was near but hadn't realized he was right behind her until he spoke. She knew it was dangerous to not pay better attention to her surroundings, but she also knew she was safe on the ship. "I'm hoping, more like wishing, we make land soon. Though, I have a feeling we have another couple more weeks to go."

Jim lightly rubbed her arms before putting his arms around her and pulling her close. Taking in both the sky and the ocean, Jim said, "Yeah, it will be. See the clouds out there?" Feeling her nod, he continued with, "Can't tell if it's starting or full force, but it's another storm. All we can hope is that by the time we get there its cleared or clearing. I'm actually glad the weather has held and that it's been relatively smooth sailing. It's been nice to not help on deck again, unless absolutely necessary."

Brandi looked up over her shoulder at him. "Since he only needed your help during that recent storm, and I'll bet he'll need it again if we're in another storm, I'll happily take it." Turning in his arms, the smile that was still on her face softened. Rising on her toes, she lightly kissed his lips before looking thoughtful and saying, "You know, if you aren't busy right now, I sure could use your help with something in our cabin."

Jim chuckled. "Really? Lead the way then, little girl. I'll be glad to help in any way possible."

Amy Allen

Chapter 11

Mid-March 1806
New Orleans, Louisiana - America

Stepping off the ship once they were docked, Brandi grinned as she looked around the riverfront. It seemed more bustling than even the port of London was. Feeling a hand on her waist, she looked up at Jim, not missing the fact he was laughing. She was more amazed at hearing not only English but also French and what she thought was a mix of French and Haitian Creole. Returning her gaze to Jim, she asked, "Do you think we have time to look around?"

Jim chuckled. There were times, like this one, that he forgot she was 42 for this lifetime and not 15 or 16. He was surprised she wasn't actually bouncing. Shrugging, as he moved slightly behind her and pulled her close, he said, "We may. I don't see Jac and Jason but that doesn't mean they haven't arrived and are in the melee – just couldn't drive whatever they are bringing any closer. Before we look around, baby, we should make sure they aren't here yet."

Brandi sighed, knowing he was right. Even though she couldn't hear it, she could feel him chuckling as she leaned her head against his chest. "Alright. Unless Andre has found them, let's go see if we can find Grann and Granpè." She didn't ask about the trunks. She knew they were safe on the ship for the time being.

Moving back to her side, Jim tucked Brandi's arm into the crook of his. As he headed them toward where he could see wagons and carriages, he had no doubt she was trying to take everything in. He could feel people staring at them as they passed by. He did what he normally didn't do and glimpsed into a mind here and there and he chuckled at the thoughts he saw. Feeling her tap a finger on his arm, Jim looked down and asked, "What?"

"That's what I was wondering. What are you laughing at?"

Returning his gaze to watching where they were going, and glancing around at the people, he chuckled again before saying, "If you hadn't noticed, people keep looking at us. Some are because of my unusual height while others are because of our difference in heights and your markings. I found, well find, the thoughts (except for those regarding how you look, which I find rude) funny." Glancing back down at her with a smile, he added, "I see Andre and Jac, but not Jason."

Brandi giggled as she shook her head. Gently chiding him, she said, "It isn't nice to intrude on others that way."

A quiet laugh rumbled through Jim's chest. "Maybe not, baby. But neither is it polite to stare."

Trying not to giggle again, Brandi rolled her eyes at Jim, giving him a mock sigh. Before she had the chance to reply, she heard, "Pitit pitit fi," from off to the side. Turning to the much-loved voice Brandi smiled. Releasing Jim's arm, she quickly moved to a woman who was a few inches taller than herself, and appeared to be in her early 70's – but was actually in her mid-90's for this lifetime they were in – with silver hair, that was partially drawn up into a bun, wearing a large hat in silk with orchids on it. Hugging the woman, Brandi grinned. "Grann! I'm glad Andre found you, but where is Granpè?"

Jim followed Brandi. Giving the older woman a grin, he said, "It's good to see you, Jacqueline. Thank you also for sending Andre to us in London."

Jacqueline Stewart hugged her granddaughter close. Focusing on Jim, she nodded to the man before saying, "It is good to see you too, Jim, and you are very welcome. Alex had not said you were with Brandi when he wrote to tell us she was headed to London. I am glad she also has had you with her. Jason and I are very happy for the two of you." Returning her attention to Brandi, Jacqueline smiled, kissed her cheek, and then said, "I am glad to see you too, child. We brought Ben with us so he and Granpè, after Ben parked the carriage among the others, managed to take the wagon closer to the ship. They will help Ken and Brian get your trunks and then Ken and Brian can ride with them home. As long as Andre doesn't mind driving the carriage, we will take the carriage home." Noticing Brandi nodding distractedly while trying to look around at what she could see of merchants on the riverfront, Jacqueline added, "We can come down tomorrow for you to look and shop. I believe I am short on some of my supplies also, so we can pick up those too."

On the way to her grandparents' home, Brandi asked, "What kind of supplies do you need?"

"I keep a variety of potions on hand. In the short time since we arrived, I have become known for my voodoo abilities so people have started to call me Mambo Jacqueline here. Even though we are more on the outskirts of town, they will find their way to the plantation for what I offer. All know I only use good magick so no voodoo dolls or black rituals or anything else like that. For specific supplies, I'm not sure what I have left on my shelves. So, I will make a list of what is needed for when we go to town tomorrow."

Brandi nodded, then thinking of something else, asked, "What about for the wedding? Is there anything in town that needs to be picked up now, or is there anything that still needs to be done?"

Jacqueline shook her head. "My house staff and I have everything under control. As long as you have your dress with you, you are done with what you need to do to help. This is your vacation."

"My dress is in a trunk carefully packed." Thinking about something her grann said, she then asked, "Your house staff?"

"Yes, our house staff. We also have workers for planting and harvesting. All are free workers and staff like Andre is a free man. We are the only ones in the area that don't have slaves. They all have papers saying they are free men and women. Jason also pays them a decent wage. The house is large and I wouldn't be able to take care of it myself. The same with the coffee fields. It is on the large side, so your Granpè needs help for taking care of it."

Brandi had been listening to her grann as she looked out the carriage window, looking at the various oaks and cypress trees they passed. Returning her attention to her grann, she said, "I guess I'm just not used to having any staff, well except Andre now. I hadn't realized people kept slaves though I had heard from a few of our friends about how there were some people that went into indentured servitude and traveled from London to America. I'm glad you don't have slaves."

The ride only took about thirty minutes. As the carriage started to turn, Brandi glanced out of the window again. She was amazed at all the oaks she saw. She then saw a sign on a post that read *Oak Hollow Plantation.* Looking down the lane they were driving up, Brandi suddenly gaped. She saw a beautiful, and large, stately two-story house with a veranda that looked to encircle both the lower and upper floors. As the carriage pulled up in front of the house and stopped, Brandi's gaze returned to her grann. "It's gorgeous."

Jacqueline gave her hand to Andre as he helped her out. Stepping to the side, she watched as Jim next stepped out before helping Brandi out. Jacqueline smiled to herself at how Andre just held the door open. "Thank you, Pitit pitit fi. We are very happy with the job Ben did for us." Noticing the wagon, she then added, "It looks like your trunks arrived and have been taken inside. Come and I'll show you around inside before taking you to your rooms."

Amy Allen

Chapter 12

March 28, 1806

Brandi sat at the vanity table finishing her hair for the ball her grandparents were holding that evening. It would be her last ball as a single woman. From what her grann mentioned, this was Mardi Gras time. She also remembered her grann mentioning celebrations for Mardi Gras, including balls, had been suspended until further notice – something about too much rowdiness – so Brandi was surprised the ball was being held. Then again, her grann had mentioned the ball wasn't necessarily for Mardi Gras but more for family and the friends her grandparents had made on neighboring plantations, as well as in town, to celebrate the wedding. Hearing a knock on the doorframe, she turned and smiled at the woman standing there. "I'm almost done, Grann."

Jacqueline Stewart smiled at her granddaughter as she stepped in the room. "It appears you still need to put your dress on, Pitit pitit fi. Your hair looks lovely, though."

Brandi giggled. "Thank you." Standing, she then asked, "Would you help me with the dress, please?"

Jacqueline had been admiring the dress. It had a high waist with a scooped neck and sleeves that were off the shoulder in a soft pink. "I'd be happy to, child. This is a beautiful gown and is perfect for tonight. Although I didn't require it, some guests may come in masks in celebration of Mardi Gras." Picking up the petticoat that lay next to the dress, Jacqueline handed it to Brandi. Once Brandi had it on, Jacqueline motioned for Brandi to turn so she could hook the garment. Jacqueline then picked the gown up and helped Brandi with pulling it over her head before Jacqueline did the ties and bow at the back. Moving to face Brandi again, Jacqueline nodded in satisfaction happy with how the coloring suited Brandi's skin tone. "You look lovely."

The house was full of people. Stepping to the ballroom door, Brandi smiled. Glancing at her grann, she said, "Are we having the wedding in here in the morning?"

Jacqueline shook her head. "No. The ceremony will be outside unless it starts to rain. We will hold the reception in here afterward, so it will stay decorated for that after the ball tonight."

"It looks amazing." Feeling a hand on her waist Brandi's face lit up at seeing Jim. "Hey there, handsome. I was just about to go looking for you."

Jim grinned first at Brandi and then at her grandmother. Leaning down, he gave Brandi a light kiss. "I was watching for you. You look stunning, baby."

Brandi nearly preened from his comments. "Thank you, love. You look rather dashing yourself." Placing her hand on his outstretched arm, Brandi walked into the ballroom with Jim, not surprised her grann was on his other side.

The ballroom was decorated for the evening, and for the next day, with beige and cream drapery type material on the walls with magnolias and orchids in pots strategically placed. Here and there were accents of black, gold, silver, green, red, and blue to give a nod to Mardi Gras without making it look like the ball was strictly for Mardi Gras. Against one wall, there was also a small orchestra containing a violinist, cellist, flutist, fortepiano player, cornet player, and timpani player all set up and ready to begin their playing. The guests milling about were dressed in their finest – friends and neighbors in costume type gowns and suits complete with masks and family in lavish gowns and formal suits without masks – while drinking Champagne. The talk around the room was of the upcoming wedding.

Finishing a dance with Jim, Brandi felt a touch to her arm. Turning, she grinned at who was standing there. "Dane! I'm so glad you're here. How did you know?"

The man Brandi called Dane stood six-feet three-inches tall with shoulder-length sandy blonde hair currently pulled back in a queue. He had known, been friends with, and even loved Brandi for the last 250 years. Because of going to see his sister Lena, or perhaps check on Lena when she was living and working at the monastery outside of St. Petersburg, Dane had found out that Brandi was being held there, and that Brandi was also pregnant. Although Brandi hadn't remembered him at the time because of the drugs she'd been given, he helped her and his sister fool Jeff, the ass that had taken Brandi, into thinking that Brandi had only one baby instead of twins and that baby was born dead. He then helped his sister with coming up with a way to have Brandi be found and rescued. Dane had been friends with Alexi, Brandi's late husband, who had been a warlock like Dane. Dane considered himself, and he knew Brandi thought the same, Brandi's warlock.

Leaning down to kiss her cheek, calling her the nickname he'd used for her since their first meeting, he said, "Of course I'm here, Angel. Nowhere else I want to be than celebrating with you. I am very happy for you and Jim. As for the how I knew, I found out from both Jim and Dominique. Before you ask, yes, I still keep in contact with Dominique."

Brandi was enjoying the ball. She not only danced with Jim, but she also danced with Dane, her uncle, her stepdad, her brothers – all that had made it, and her Granpè. Finishing a dance with Jim, she walked with him back to where they had left their glasses of Champagne. Taking a sip of hers, she then stood on her toes, gave Jim a light kiss, and said, "I'll be right back. I need to run upstairs briefly." Her Champagne seemed to taste slightly off, but she attributed it to sitting for so long while she was dancing.

Jim had the urge to pull her close but refrained after the light kiss. "Is everything alright, baby?"

Brandi nodded. "It's fine. I just want to go up and check my hair. Grann said it was starting to come down in back. I am also getting warm in here with all these people."

Jim drew her in slightly before dipping down to give her another kiss. "All right. I'll try to keep from following you up. How about a walk in the garden when you come back down?"

Brandi smiled at him. "A walk sounds wonderful. I'll hurry." Making sure she had her glass, Brandi left the room.

Jim watched her leave. Having the feeling something was off, he almost went back on his word and followed her. Looking around the room, he found the one person he knew would help if needed. Catching the other man's eye, he motioned toward the front foyer. Stepping out of the ballroom, he moved to stand near the stairs next to the man already there. "Thanks for joining me out here, Dane. Did you see her leave to head upstairs? Something is wrong but it's like she's blocking or something else is."

"No problem. I did see her. Agreed, something is wrong, but I'm not sure what it is either. I'd suggest we stay out here to see if she needs any help without going up to check on her," Dane said. He wasn't surprised Jim only sighed and nodded.

Getting upstairs, Brandi walked into her room and looked around wondering why she was there. Taking a larger sip of Champagne, she noticed her head felt foggy and she felt ... well, she wasn't quite sure. Placing her glass on a little table just inside her bedroom door, she moved to her vanity and sat.

Finishing with fixing the area that was coming down, glad she'd secured her hair fairly well from the start, Brandi started to stand when she suddenly had to sit again. Her head was starting to hurt causing her to rest it briefly. Feeling a need to have more of her Champagne, her glass was in her hand with only a thought. Brandi noticed her glass looked full again but just shrugged, figuring she had drunk less then she'd realized. The off taste that had been there earlier seemed more pronounced now as well as familiar but she couldn't quite put her finger on where she'd come across it before. Hearing a very familiar laugh, one she hated, from the doorway caused her to quickly look up toward the door.

He had been watching her, as well as that idiot he'd overheard she was marrying. He'd already killed one husband, so another would be no problem. When he followed her upstairs, he had also noticed the brother of that bitch Lena. If he had the chance he'd kill that asshole too. First, he needed to remind this little whore just who she belonged to. When he'd heard about this little soiree, hearing that guests could wear masks made him happy. No one who knew him would recognize him with the mask he'd chosen.

He could see her drugged drink was taking effect. He wanted her pliable and forgetful, but not passed out. Standing at the door, he couldn't help but laugh at her predicament. Behind his mask he smiled at the look on her face when she heard him and her head turned to him. Stepping in, he said, "I see you're whoring yourself out to someone else." Reaching her he pulled her head back. "Looks like I need to remind you who you actually belong to, you whoring bitch."

Brandi tried to pull her head back, hoping to release his grip. She'd found out when he'd grabbed her, Lexi, and Lexi's brother and sister after Brandi had gotten out of the monastery, that he got off if she showed she was in any pain when he hurt her. Trying to keep her emotions in check, she only said, "Jeff." Sending a message to Jim, knowing he would be wondering why he was getting an off feeling from her followed by fear and pain, she only said ~Help.~

He laughed more. "Good, you remember. But, even though you've been hiding, it hasn't been that long." Not liking that she was trying to get out of his grip, he made a fist and backhanded her with it as he pulled her to her feet. Eyeing the front of her dress, he tossed her to the bed. Before Jeff had the chance to take another step, he was suddenly grabbed from behind.

Jim, with Dane close behind, had already been heading upstairs when he heard Brandi say Help in his mind. Getting to her room, he nearly let his tiger loose, but barely kept it in check – only a growl escaping his lips. He lifted Jeff off his feet and threw him toward Dane as he continued to where Brandi was sprawled on the bed. At a quick glance, Jim could see her dress was still in one piece and that there only seemed to be a bruise starting to form on her left cheek. Sitting down and drawing her to him, he quietly asked, "Are you all right, baby?"

Dane caught Jeff easily and grinned menacingly, "Bet you didn't think you'd see me again. I told you what I'd do to you if you ever hurt her again." He was glad to see Jeff looking frightened. Looking at Jim and Brandi, he said, "I'm going to take out the trash. I'll see you both downstairs later, if you manage to return to the ball." Dane was wishing he had a way to kill Jeff, but, unfortunately, he didn't. It was something he'd have to talk to Brandi about.

Jim only nodded to Dane, his focus still on Brandi. "Baby?"

Brandi drew her head back so she was looking at Jim, tears now sliding down her face. "I'm fine. He only hit me."

Jim let go of the breath he hadn't realized he was holding. He'd feared the worst but was glad those fears hadn't happened. Needing to know something else, he then asked, "Do you want to put tomorrow off for a few days or so?"

Brandi smiled at him before leaning back in to lightly kiss him. Shaking her head, she replied, "No. I've waited too many years as it is. I want to marry you tomorrow as planned. For this evening though, I want to get rid of my glass of Champagne since I think he put something in it, and then rest up here. I know Grann may get upset, but I'd rather you not leave. If you need to let her know though, please come back up to sit with me."

Pulling her closer, understanding why she didn't want to go back down that evening but very glad she didn't want to put the wedding off, Jim only nodded. He actually had no doubt two of her brothers would be up shortly to check on her since they would have felt her get hurt too.

Amy Allen

Chapter 13

March 29, 1806

Brandi woke feeling safe and secure. Snuggling in, she noticed the arms around her tighten slightly as she felt a combination of a growl and a laugh rumble through the chest her head was resting on. Tilting her head back, she looked up at Jim. "Good morning, handsome. I'm glad Grann let you stay."

Leaning down, Jim kissed the top of her head before pulling her back close. Chuckling more, he calmed some before saying, "Morning, baby. After I told her what happened and that you asked me to stay, she agreed that my being here with you was the best choice. His showing up made me think of this last night but you were already falling asleep when I came back up. Do you have your Katana here or is it still in London?"

Brandi smiled at the question even though she'd forgotten about it. Leaning back to be able to look at him again, she said, "I have it here. I managed to get it into one of the trunks. I hate to say it, but I actually didn't even remember I brought it with me until you just asked. I wasn't in any frame of mind last night to grab it, nor did I have the chance."

Bringing her back to him and resting his head on hers, he only nodded in response. He didn't even want to think what would have happened if he and Dane hadn't gotten upstairs as quick as they did.

Rubbing Brandi's back through her chemise, Jim quietly held her for a few minutes before saying, "I love you, Bree. I know I haven't been around as much to protect you as I should have, but that doesn't mean I haven't known what's going on with you. The only times I didn't was for the two years that brother and sister had you in their castle in 1197 and then the six years that asshole had you in the monastery. So when Dominique notified me about finding out where you were and what she wanted me to do, I took every short cut I could to get back but it still took longer than I wanted so Adam, Gray, and Lexi beat me to it. As much as I wanted it to be me that found you, I'm glad they did and got the rest of Dominique's plan in motion. As you know, I stayed close by in Russia, since that day nearly 27 years ago even though you and Lexi were together. Even if we weren't where we were now and Lexi was still alive, I would still be staying close and I'd still love you. But, Lexi isn't alive and, I thank the gods we are where we are now so you may find I'm even more protective than I have been. It may take so much more to kill either of us, but he can still hurt you. That not only hurts me, but it also pisses me off."

Jim could tell he was getting worked up when he felt her hand run across his chest as if she was helping him calm and letting him know everything was fine. Smiling into her hair at the gesture, he then asked, "How's your face feeling this morning?"

Brandi listened to all Jim had to say. She knew part of why he hadn't been close was because until Jeff had taken her and Josh out of their front yard, she hadn't thought she needed his or his brothers' protection. She had a handle on that dark side of herself – the reason they had been asked to watch out for and protect her all those millennia ago. She was glad he hadn't been that far since she and Joshua left the monastery. Part of her even wished it had been him that saw her outside, even if she knew she wouldn't have remembered who he was at that time. Too many of those memories were still lost to her. At his last question she tilted her head so he could hear, and, leaving that part for the moment, said, "First, I love you too, Jim. I would love you even if we hadn't gotten to where we are now. I also thank the gods that we are where we are now and I also know you'll be more protective from this point on. And for that, I'm very glad. I can only think of two other times I've ever really been scared and he tops those by so much more. I don't think you've ever seen him, so you wouldn't have known who he was in general, but Dane has seen him and even he wouldn't have recognized him downstairs. He had a mask so he could be able to blend in with Grann's friends. I'm glad you got there when you did."

Quietly sighing, she lifted a hand to her face and cheek. "It aches. It may be bruised, but I'm sure I can find something to cover it up for today." Starting to sit up on her elbow to show him, she heard a knock. Glancing to the door, she called out, "Come in."

Jacqueline stepped into the room, smiling at the couple. "It's time to get up and get ready. This means you will need to return to your room now, Jim. Just let Alex or Ben know if you need anything. You will see Brandi in a couple of hours."

Knowing it was better to not argue with Jacqueline, even if he was technically older than her, Jim gave Brandi a kiss before getting up and leaving the room.

Returning her gaze to her granddaughter after seeing Jim exit, Jacqueline watched Brandi roll over and sit up on the edge of the bed. Noticing Brandi's face, she sat down next to Brandi. "Oh, Pitit pitit fi. I'm so sorry, but that bruise looks nasty. I think I have something in my supplies that will help it heal. In the meantime, I have some face powder that we can use to lighten it. Help it blend in better with your markings. You have time for a bath if you'd like."

"A bath sounds wonderful. What do you have to help the bruise? And will it help it stop hurting?" Brandi wondered.

"I have a solution I made from Witch Hazel. I have a cloth that I use for it. I'll put some on the bruise with the cloth while you bathe."

It was a beautiful day, allowing the wedding to take place outside. When it was time, Brandi headed downstairs with her grandmother to await her dad, Alex.

Brandi's dress was in a soft pink. It had a high waist with a scoop neck and long lacey sleeves from the upper arm down, fitting closer at the wrists. It also had a short train in back. The hat she wore was also in the same pink. Although it wasn't a current norm, she had lace, which could be pulled down over her face, attached to the front of the hat as a veil. Though her face still ached, the bruise now wasn't as noticeable because of the powder her grann had applied to her cheek. Because of how long her hair was, her grann had drawn the majority of it up into an intricate braid and knot with some tendrils hanging loosely around her face.

Taking her dad's arm, she smiled up at the man. He wasn't her dad by blood, nor had he ever adopted her and her two brothers, but she had considered him dad for more years than she could think of.

Alex smiled down at Brandi. For him, she was his daughter – as her brothers Mike and Eric were his sons – and had been for several millennia. Looking at her now, he wished her mother, his late wife Danielle, was still alive to see Brandi as happy as she was. "You look beautiful, sweetheart. I don't just mean the way you look in that lovely dress. Even despite our uninvited guest last night, your happiness at marrying Jim shines through. I wish your mother was able to see you now."

Returning his smile, Brandi nodded. "Thank you. I wish she were here, but I have a feeling Momma can see me, Daddy."

Alex patted her hand. "Ready?"

Brandi closed her eyes briefly, taking a deep breath and letting it out slowly. Raising her gaze back to Alex, she only gave a small inclination of her head to let him know she was.

The walk down the aisle to Jim felt like the longest walk she'd ever taken. Reaching him, she stepped to his side, placing her hand on his arm when her dad lifted it off his own arm and held her hand out to Jim. She smiled up at Jim, love shining in her eyes, thinking he looked more handsome than ever. She was glad she told him that she didn't want to put it off when he'd asked the night before.

As he watched Brandi come to him, Jim found his throat was suddenly dry. Even though she was the most beautiful woman he'd ever seen and he hadn't thought there would be a moment he would think her even more lovely, he knew he was wrong. He thought she was even more beautiful now from her love for him and happiness at their joining that seemed to radiate from her. To him, their happiness and love for each other felt palpable.

In front of their families, as well as friends and neighbors of her grandparents, they exchanged their simple vows and then they exchanged rings. He had told her back when they were first engaged, when she'd asked, that he would be happy to go against social norms by wearing a ring when the time came. They stood close, hands linked, as the minister finished the ceremony before Jim lifted her veil and leaned down to lightly kiss her while showing her promises of what was yet to come. After the kiss, the minister looked out at the guests and said, "I now present to you, Mr. and Mrs. James Richards." Hearing that, Brandi bit her lip to keep from laughing. Knowing his given name was Jim and not James and that he actually had no last name, it was strange to hear him called James with a last name. From next to her, she heard the start of a chuckle quickly covered by a cough.

As they walked back down the aisle together, Brandi noticed her grandmother get up from her seat to meet them. Knowing there was a wedding lunch prior to the afternoon ball for the reception, Brandi and Jim followed Jacqueline in with the rest of the guests following them to the formal dining room, sitting where they were instructed.

As Jim pulled her chair out for her, he leaned close to quietly say, "We'll need to sign the certificate after we eat. Jason asked the minister to stay for lunch before heading back to town. He said he would only stay if we make sure to sign directly after we are done, before we head into the reception."

Brandi nodded and said, "I'm glad he agreed to stay for lunch and that's fine." She wasn't surprised her grandfather had maneuvered it to where the minister would agree to stay and eat.

As soon as everyone was seated, lunch was served by the kitchen staff. Unlike the wedding ceremony, it was lively around the table with conversations and laughter flowing as freely as the wine.

Once lunch was done, the cake was brought out. It was a two-layered fruit cake covered in white frosting with magnolia blossoms on the top. After removing the flowers, since they were not edible, Brandi and Jim cut the first slice of cake. Putting it on a plate, they shared it and fed it to each other, as Jacqueline cut the rest of the cake and passed it to the guests. After everyone finished their slice and got up from the table, Brandi and Jim moved to where the minister was now standing so they could sign what they needed to while the guests congregated in the ballroom. After they were through signing what the minister had for them, and had thanked the minister before escorting him to the door and wishing him a safe ride back to town, Brandi and Jim joined everyone.

The reception ball was like the ball the night before with Brand first dancing with Jim and then dancing with her grandfather, dad, uncle, and brothers while Jim danced with her grandmother, as well as Brandi's daughters, Anna and Leah. Brandi and Jim also made sure to make the rounds getting congratulations from all the guests. As it was during lunch, conversations and laughter flowed but instead of wine, everyone was drinking Champagne.

As the ball started to wind down, Jim and Brandi made their rounds again, thanking the friends and neighbors for coming. Having already been informed that Jim could move into Brandi's room after the wedding, and ready to start their wedding night, they then thanked her grandparents for hosting the festivities before they quietly left the ball to head upstairs.

Knowing it'd be quicker if he just carried her Jim swept Brandi up into his arms and bounded up the stairs. Getting into what was now their room, he kicked the door closed before he set her back on her feet and taking her into his arms. Very shortly they had rid each other of their wedding clothes and fell to the bed locked together, knowing they were in for a long and wild night.

About Author

I was born and raised in California, and in early 2007 moved to Reno, Nevada. Besides writing, I am a Licensed Practical Nurse (LPN) and have been since early 1989. I have been working as a home care nurse, mostly Pediatric, since 2004 and have been in my current position since moving to Reno.

When not working, I love to write - I have been writing for at least 17 years but only became published in mid-2016 - and, over the years I have completed several fanfictions as well as some original stories, which I didn't think of publishing the original ones at the time. However, I now have several published works – a few are clean contemporary/historical paranormal romances, but most are sexily erotic contemporary/historical paranormal romances.

For this year (and on), I have several works in progress, some with Brandi and others featuring new characters – including at least a couple fantasy ones (I plan on one of those fantasy ones being a many book series), and at least one sci-fi (both with Brandi and new characters). All will be paranormal romances – though the multi-book series won't start out as romance.

When I'm not writing - I read (or I try to), I spend time with my cats, watch TV/movies, and play an online vampire game.

More Books by Amy:

Novels/Novellas –

The Many Lives of Brandi Series:

A Love Ignited: The Many Lives of Brandi Series Book 1
Love Can Find a Way: The Many Lives of Brandi Series Book 4
Surprises: The Many Lives of Brandi Series Book 5 (Currently unpublished for major updates)
The Aftermath: The Many Lives of Brandi Series Book 6
A Heart Recognized: The Many Lives of Brandi Series Book 7 - the Texas Saga 1
Second Chances: The Many Lives of Brandi Series Book 8 - The Vampire and Her Wolf Saga 1
Holiday Fun: The Many Lives of Brandi Series - The Vampire and Her Wolf Saga 2
For The Love of St. Nick: The Many Lives of Brandi Series Book 9

Girl and the Fireman Series:

New Beginnings
Holiday Surprises
Masquerade Gone Awry
Simmering Illusions

Omnibus/Boxed sets:

The Girl and the Fireman: The Complete Series

Made in the USA
Middletown, DE
07 January 2023

18005220R10059